"Satan, the father of lies, blesses people with guns and drugs to play with as toys. The puppet master addicts and controls- blinding the eyes with these toys that destroy lives."

-REDRUM DA REAPER-

ACKNOWLEDGEMENTS

First and foremost, I would like to acknowledge that my inspiration for this book is a gift from God. All glory and honor is His! This book is dedicated to my moms. I could not have completed this project without you. Thank you for helping me prove that I'm more than just a gangsta. Now I'm an author, thanks to you!

Also to, my daughter "L-Silly" I know life is MESSY and God willing we can get to know each other better soon. I love you mija!

Also to my "Memo" I lost my life before you were born, but your life is proof that I did something right when I was free. I love you mijo.

Last, but surely not least, to my true love LC. You bring out the worst and best in me. I hate that you always keep your love out of my reach. All ain't fair in love and war.

All four of you have motivated me in one way or another, to put down and release this high power banger! Thank you! God bless you all.

CRUCIFIX

Contents

PROLOGUE
(NOVEMBER 1984, THE CITY OF COLTON)

The Rose Garden Apartments on the north side of Colton were straight ghetto and grimy. They were a complex of 500 blue and off-white in color, low budget, run-down, HUD Section-8 living quarters. A quarter of the apartments were abandoned and had no running water or electricity. That didn't stop the gangsters and drug dealers from turning them into dope houses. Then the dope fiend addicts turned the other ones into slamming galleries or places to smoke dope and drink alcohol. The complex landlord even accepted drugs as payment for rent. Yes, but only after the sly, slick and wicked drug dealers intentionally got him hooked on a mega potent bomb batch of speed that literally turned Mr. Landlord into a meth monster.

More than a few murder victims, suicide victims and overdosed dope fiends were hauled out of the Rose Garden Apartments in an ambulance or hearse every month. Homeless bums and winos loitered the area as well, searching for a place to rest.

The North Colton gangsters were somewhat militant and organized when it came down to protecting their turf. The dealers' dope houses were all the way at the back of the complex. There were three lines of defense that a customer had to pass through just to *score*. This tight defensive circle was really intact just to short stop any jackers or robbers who might want to rob a dope connection. Some of these dealers had Mexican Mafia ties and were selling dope for mob members in Pelican Bay and Corcoran SHU (Security Housing Unit) and could not afford to fall victim to a 211-robbery, because as greedy as the Mafia is, their dealers could fall victim to a 187-murder if they didn't come correct with the mob member. This is why security was so tight knit.

The first front liners were the *little homies,* still looking innocent and young. They didn't tote any guns. Their job was to act as *lookouts*...keeping point. The little homies had one type of whistle to alert when the police were approaching the complex, so dealers could quickly disappear, shutting down shop, stashing all the guns and drugs so as not to chop a loss.

The lookouts had a second style of whistle to alert all the homies, gangsters, riders and gunmen of approaching enemies on the prowl, creeping and crawling, looking for trouble. This was gang banging, so when trouble came knocking, the Colton G's answered the door when needed. The second and third line of defense would run to the little homies' aid on the front lines, bringing up the rear, and then all everyone would hear were neighborhood gang names being yelled out, nines sparking, twelve gages bucking, sks and M1 carbines spitting assault rifle bullets, followed by cursing. This was the hood. The second and third lines of defense were seriously strapped up with weapons-AK47's and nine millimeter Uzis with one in the chamber and with the safety off. The guards were scattered twenty to thirty yards in distance, so when Funk season jumped, they had the spot sewed up and every soldier had each other's back. No cowards allowed in this camp. Every G ran to danger, flirting with death, while every kid and law-abiding citizen ran away for cover and safety.

Rules were set in this hood and they applied to everyone, gang members or not. The number one rule was what the Italian Mafia calls *Omerta,* the code of silence. This applied with the Raza as well. NO SNITCHING! The dealers posted, slanging speed, weed, crack and heroin. No kids were allowed to play in the back area. It was a dangerous fast paced, one way in one way out, death trap for any outsiders there with hidden agendas or under false pretenses. By pushing this tight structure, the hood was sewed up and on lock. It was under control of the G's from every corner to all movement in the immediate area.

Holding down the fort was mandatory. Backing each other up was mandatory. When it came to banging the rule was shoot first, ask questions later. There was a cold-blooded gang and drug war in full effect, cracking in the hood. Poisonous dope and hard drugs infested the city of Colton like rats and roaches infest a dumpsite. It was all bad. The treacherous sounds of rapid gunfire echoed through the night and even in broad daylight at times. This life became the normal everyday activity for someone growing up in the Rose Garden

Apartments.

This was home to a young, good kid named Tito Lopez. At eleven years old, Tito learned to ignore the gunshots in the distance; however, he would instinctively duck and flinch whenever shots rang out in close range in his complex. He quickly learned to avoid flying stray bullets, headhunting for a target. He was lucky. Others were not so lucky and learned that lesson the hard way. Tito's best friend, Alex Lara, for example, lost his little brother Jesse Lara to a stray bullet. I guess that's what they mean when they say '*bullets have no names*'. Tito witnessed Jesse's accidental murder. Jesse's terrified screams haunted and chased Tito in his dreams at night. Nightmarish lost souls and murdered ghosts haunted his playground. *The devils playground*, as nicknamed by the hood's riders.

Tito was a young street-smart survivor. His life though, was a never-ending struggle. He was sometimes depressed, wondering why he even tried to stay alive. He hated his life. That wasn't even the worst part either. Tito's family was dirt poor and to add insult to injury, both his parents were drug addicts. It seemed his father Erik Lopez was more worried about getting high than about his own son's well-being. Erik was a scumbag, lowdown and dirty. Tito's mother Denise on the other hand, loved and cared for her son the best way she knew how. But she was controlled by fear. Erik scared her terribly. Denise smoked weed and speed and was an alcoholic. She was a half-decent parent, unlike Erik, the cold-hearted piece of shit heroin addict.

Tonight Tito stood outside holding a soccer ball staring at the police helicopter, also known as the *ghetto bird,* circling above him. The bright light flashed down upon him and the surrounding area, searching the dark for criminals and possible suspects. All the kids were still out and playing a game of tag. The low helicopter got their attention as they acted as if the cops were hunting for them. They ran and they scattered as the game of tag became a game of cops and robbers. Gangsters and drug dealers nonchalantly slid into their homes. The kids pretended to be the hoods gangsters and drug dealers trying to escape from the police.

Many of these kids didn't have positive role models so the gangsters became their role models. The G's were looked up to as neighborhood heroes, as protectors, as the ones who wouldn't let any outsiders hurt them or their families. The sad part was ninety percent of these kids would really be running from the cops in a few years, becoming part of the lost youth. You could say it was their fate to become a gangster or drug dealer, or worse, a drug addict enslaved by the gangster, dealer and criminal cultures.

They were born into the cycle. *Trapped* in the cycle. They'd eventually be trapped in the jail system, and when they'd parole, be trapped in the barrio, Stuck in the hood. Forever trapped in the deadly web of violence. Yes, where they see and hear evil, but are trained not to speak of that evil. They would just accept that this was life and they'd pray the evil didn't happen to them.

Little Tito was different from most of his friends. He always stood out from the rest. When the helicopter lights flashed down upon him, he didn't run. He innocently stood there daydreaming, staring up in awe and smiling and waving at the ghetto bird. Tito wished he could be a Colton cop. He wished that he could be flying the helicopter, patrolling the skies and stalking the streets from above like an eagle, hunting down the bad guys and crooks. Tito especially hated the drug dealers. He blamed dealers for his dysfunctional family. He wanted to arrest a dealer by the name of Veneno from San Bernardino who had gotten his father hooked on heroin. In Tito's mind, Veneno ruined his family.

Tito was a slim 120-pound kid. 5'6," short brown slicked back hair, with an upside down heart shaped scar under his right eye. Today he wore white baggy sport shorts and a black t-shirt with red letters across the chest that read *D.A.R.E. to keep kids off drugs.* He had gotten this t-shirt when the Colton PD gave a drugs and alcohol presentation at his elementary school. Officers spoke on the dangers of drugs and even showed the students drugs and paraphernalia. Tito was all too familiar with these dangers, being that his parents were addicts, and he was therefore surrounded by the contraband on a daily basis.

Tito prayed he would wake up out of his nightmarish life one day and be living his lifelong dream of being a cop. Tito was eleven now, so he had just seven years until his eighteenth birthday, at which time he would join the academy. He planned to join that very day he turned eighteen, if he lived that long. At the presentation officer Garza, a rookie, made all the kids honorary Jr. Officers. All the kids received plastic CPD badges. Tito was proud of his CPD badge and honorary status. He took his status seriously. You can even say he took it to the heart to where he appointed himself Jr. Cop duties. The gangsters patrolled their hood at night, and so did little Tito. He was faithful to his duties, with his plastic badge attached over his heart. He carried a little flashlight and every night at six p.m. he would pick up empty drug baggies, broken glass pipes and syringes. He didn't want any of the smaller kids to stumble across the paraphernalia and get sick or hurt.

While he was at it, he would collect bottles and cans to recycle. That was his legit little hustle. Sometimes those bottles and cans were the only reason he got to eat sopas that night. Of course, Tito would share what little food he hustled with his hungry friends who had it much worse than him. Tito thought it was his duty to protect the smaller kids from bullies even though he wasn't that big himself. The kid was a brave heart. He was sincere and had a heart of gold as well as a very sharp and aware mind for his age. Tito probably would become that ten percent that would escape the barrio, doing something productive with his life, avoiding becoming just another sad statistic. He was a fighter who took more than a few beatings sticking up for the smaller weaker kids in his complex or at school. He was a rough neck, tough kid who showed no fear even when he was terrified.

The helicopter circled closer, lights flashing off and on, then off it went to another area. Little Eddie was a red blur in Tito's peripheral vision as the game of tag resumed. Tito felt a slap tag, snapping him out of his daydream.

He heard Eddie shout, "You're it, ha-ha, you're it Tito!"

Eddie hid behind an open dumpster taunting his friend, "You can't catch me ha-ha!"

Tito spotted his best friend Alex Lara and his first love Tina who were closest to him. Both were hiding behind a stolen burnt Cadillac. Tina broke wide sprinting across the dry yellow grass. She was Tito's target. He ran off after her, as a hungry speeding cheetah goes after its prey. Tito had had a crush on Tina ever since she had given him his first French kiss during a game of 'Hide and Go Get It'.

'Hide and Go Get It' is a game much like 'Hide and Go Seek' but with a hood twist. The girls hide and the boys seek out the girls they want to kiss or fool around with. Yes sir, the boys 'gots to go get it, get it', hence came the name of the game. Tito's best friend Alex also liked Tina so he would always try to find her, but she would hide good and only let herself be found by Tito.

Tina had light brown curly hair flowing to the middle of her back. She was 5'7" and had tan brown skin and green eyes. At age thirteen, she was already maturing quickly and her figure was filling out nicely. All the boys teased her but secretly liked her. She was wearing white shorts and a baby blue tank top.

Tito caught up to Tina, giving her booty a quick light tag. Tito smiled and giggled as he enjoyed his cheap thrill hollering, "You're it Tina! You're it girl!"

Tina spun in her tracks accidentally slipping on a loose piece of glass. She screamed in pain, falling, and then holding on to a scraped knee. Tito felt bad, turned and ran to her side, putting his hand on her knee.

"Tina, are you okay?" he asked.

She instinctively pulled away. "No it burns, it's bleeding," she said.

Tito took off his shirt, wrapped it around her knee and put his arm around her protectively. Little Eddie, Dannyboy, Terri, Jessica, Alex, and Maryjane quit playing and jogged over to Tina and Tito.

"Tito, hurry give Tina mouth to mouth resesitipitation! Ha-ha! Give her mouth to mouth hurry!" Jessica playfully said.

The young crowd teased and laughed, bumping elbows and throwing kisses at one another, average child's play.

Tito wasn't amused though, in fact, he was upset and his cheeks were turning red. He didn't think anything was funny when he said, "It's mouth to mouth resuscitation not resesitipitation you dumb ass idiot. Why don't you all shut the hell up! She's hurt! Ain't nothin funny man!"

Dannyboy smirked and laughed saying, "You swear Tito, who you think you are captain save-a-hoe or what?"

Tito gave him a mean-mug. If looks could kill, Dannyboy would be dead. Looking at him with the evil eye, Tito jumped at Dannyboy who took off running, scared as hell.

Tito hollered, "That's what I thought. You're the hoe, lil foolio, lil pussy!"

The crowd got serious now as Tina whined when Tito lifted her up and headed towards his apartment. What few lights that actually worked in the complex turned on. In the distance rapid gunfire rang out. Death was in the air, proving that the Grim Reaper wasn't a myth, but did truly exist and was stalking the hood for lives. Then the wicked sick demons from the fiery pits of hell would appear to collect lost souls and drag them down to the throne of the prince of darkness.

Little Eddie and Terri shot at each other with their fingers when they heard the shots up the block. Then their imaginary guns went into their waistbands, copying the G's stilo of concealing their weapons. These two kids idolized the gangsters, especially one leader named Redrum. He was considered the 'Big Homie' and was treated with the utmost respect. He was known for doing dirt, putting down murders for his hood, committed to winning this barrio warfare he was wrapped up in. He was the type of OG who would give out dollar bills and buy all the kids' ice cream when the ice cream truck rolled into the complex. He was feared, even hated and despised by some. Little Eddie and Terri tried walking, talking and acting like him.

Just then, Rum cruised by in a murder black El Camino lowrider, dressed on chrome Dayton's. He was heading to the dope house in the back to open shop. He waved at Tito and Tina throwing up the peace sign, hitting switches in the tight lowrider, which made it bounce up and down. He had loud music, straight gangster rap, bumping out of the speakers in the back of the truck.

Tina was limping with her arm around Tito's shoulder. He held her up and tried to comfort her saying, "My mom will clean you up Tina, don't worry."

Tina blushed and winked at her best friend Jessica because she was getting a crutch hug from Tito. She felt puppy love for Tito and thought; *a scraped knee is worth a little special attention and hugs from Tito*. Jessica elbowed Terri, holding in a laugh, covering her mouth.

Tito's mom Denise was in her half empty apartment in front of the stove trying to relight her joint. It was the bombest weed going through the Inland Empire and she was already high. She toked it and then held it deep in her lungs, but it was too much for her because she began choking as she exhaled the potent Indica smoke.

She heard her son Tito yelling for her help, "Mom help! Tina slipped and cut her knee on a broken 40 bottle."

Denise pushed aside the dirty, torn, off-white yellowish sheet she used as a curtain and saw her son outside carrying his little girlfriend. She opened the dusty screen door for them as they both stumbled in and sat on the filthy orange couch.

Denise toked her joint, asking her son, "Shit what the hell you kids doing out there man, throwing glass at each other?"

A big cloud of bud smoke filled the room and Tina waved it towards the open door.

Just then, Lil Eddie and Dannyboy strolled through the door, right into the smoke. They both inhaled deeply waving the weed smoke into their own faces, looking like a mini version of Cheech-n-Chong. They were laughing and Lil Eddie said, "Damn it! Smell that shit D-Boy! That's that bomb yeska huh?"

Dannyboy kept smelling and fanning the smoke answering, "Yeah man fo chingy! I think it's that sticky icky my dad's slangin. He's getting his ball on off that shit huh Denise?"

Dannyboy then began smoking an imaginary joint and passed it to Alex's little square ass who walked onto the scene. Alex didn't play along though, so little Eddie grabbed the imaginary joint saying, "Pass that shit fool, puff-puff pass. Muthafuckin give fool, break mines off dawg."

They both giggled as Denise put her roach out and stepped on it, swatting at the foolish acting boys. She shouted, "Oh my God, you guys are retarded! Shut your stupid asses up. All you lil traviesos mind your own business and take your lil weed smokin asses home!"

Dannyboy tried to pick up the rest of Denise's joint, but she slapped his hand away. "Stop D-boy, I'm gonna tell your mom."

Dannyboy answered, "She don't care."

Denise realized he was right. "Yeah you're right, she used to smoke weed when she was pregnant with you, now look at you."

Dannyboy threw a punch in the air at Denise saying, "Look at me? Look at you-you fuckin stoner! You spend all your money on weed, there ain't even no food in this shack."

Denise was examining Tina's knee and answered, "That reminds me, go ask your mom if I can borrow ten dollars in food stamps and a couple cigarettes."

Dannyboy bounced his soccer ball on his knee saying, "Naw, it's alright, you go ask her, I'm not your slave." Denise swung at Dannyboy and grabbed his little rattail but he slipped away hollering, "Too slow hoe, too slow hoe."

Tito heard his friend disrespect his mom and jumped up furiously, nose and forehead wrinkled and fist clenched. Tito knuckled up to teach D-boy a lesson about respect. Dannyboy had called Tina a hoe a few minutes ago, now he had called Denise a hoe. That was it. He had crossed the line. Tito ran towards Dannyboy but D-boy threw his ball in Tito's face, slowing him down as they ran out of the house. Tito's adrenaline rush and anger made him shake off the hit and he hook-kicked D-boy's leg, dropping him to the asphalt.

Tito kicked him in the ass a few times, hovering over him yelling, "Don't ever talk to my mom's like that, Tina either! If you do I'm gonna mop you up and not stop you lil bastard! I'm tired of you fools acting stupid!"

D-boy turned over putting his hands up to block any punches Tito might throw. D-boy's hands were cut from the asphalt and his pride made him yell, "Whatever man!"

Tito yelled back in a dead serious tone, "What do you mean whatever? You think I'm playing? Get up fool! I won't kick you while you're down. Get up! I'll give you a one-on-one fair fight. Get up!"

D-boy stayed on the ground, frozen. He'd never seen Tito this mad or this serious. He smirked and got up slowly, dusting himself off. He bent down to tie his shoe.

Tina yelled out from the apartment, "Stop fighting you guys!"

Tito turned towards her and D-boy saw his opportunity and took it, trying to sucker punch Tito. Tito ducked and punched D-boy dead on his nose, watering his eyes and hollering, "Too slow hoe!"

D-boy's nose was leaking blood. That's all it took for him to kneel, bowing down in surrender.

Tito said, "You better learn something about respect boy. You're my friend and I don't like fucking you up, but you deserve a ass kicking! Quit playing and we'll be all good."

Little Eddie stood close by and said, "Kick back Tito, Lala's crawling towards you and she's scared."

Tito looked behind him and saw his baby sister Zoe-LaLa looking up at him. He picked her up and gave her a big hug and little kisses. That made her giggles with excitement. She was wearing nothing but a diaper.

Tito walked inside, shutting the door on his friends. Little Eddie kicked the soccer ball across the parking lot and the game resumed as the kids chased the ball. Tito gave Zoe-LaLa some snack crackers while Denise worked on stopping the bleeding on Tina's knee.

"This ain't that bad mija. There's no glass in it. You should be all right. Thank you for chin-checking D-boy Tito, he was fucking up my high," said Denise.

Tito rolled his eyes. He didn't like his mom getting high.

"D-boy calls everyone hoe because his mom's a hoe. That puta's always selling her wonga panocha for a shot of dope! Pinche cochina. She don't even know who his real dad is," Denise said.

Tito bounced his sixteen-month-old sister Zoe-LaLa on his knee. She giggled the whole time imagining she was on a pony.

Tito loved his little baby sister, but she wasn't his blood sister. Zoe-Lala's real mom was a dope fiend prostitute who hung out in the Rose Garden complex with anyone who had dope and wanted to fuck. She was passed around like a joint from pad to pad, and the sad part was that Zoe-LaLa was always there in the mix. Her mom had no shame in her game.

Tito was playing with his sister remembering the day he stumbled across baby Zoe-LaLa.

It had been five months or so ago, and that evening Tito was patrolling the complex like clockwork. He was in and out of apartments collecting cans and bottles when he heard deep cries from a baby in the apartment next door, which was an abandoned slamming gallery. Tito turned on his flashlight carefully walking through the dope spot. The cries got louder, and all of a sudden he saw the baby. She was dirty, smelling like piss and shit. She was crawling over her mother's dead body. Her mother had a syringe sticking out of her arm and she was purple, reeking of death, an obvious overdose of heroin. Her pockets were inside out, which meant someone probably ran across the baby and her dead mother, checked her pockets and left, robbing her of what little she had.

Zoe-LaLa had mocos running down her nose and was crying over her mom's dead body, "Mama, mama, mama."

Tito's eyes teared up when he saw her. The scene broke his heart. Situations like this reminded Tito why he never wanted to get high or do drugs. Tito took the baby home to his mother and father.

What happened next was total insanity and unheard of. Tito's greedy father Erik came up with the outrageous idea of keeping the baby so they could somehow someway collect welfare checks! He wanted to use that money to buy more heroin.

An anonymous phone call was made and Zoe-Lala's mom's dead body was taken away. Police investigated, half-assed, but like always, no one knew or saw anything. The Rose Gardens residents knew Denise and Erik kept the baby and kept their secret. They figured the baby at least had a home now and Denise wasn't much worse than Zoe-Lala's real mother was so they let sleeping dogs lay.

This is how Tito ended up with a little sister. Tito loved her on sight and spent his free time taking care of her and playing with her, making sure she had been clean and never neglected. Tito vowed to protect his baby sister with his own life. She shared his bed and he would sing her songs and tell her stories at night.

Her favorite song was a song by the Delfonics called, "LaLa Means I Love You."[i] She used to try to sing the lyrics but all she could say was LaLa and mumble. That's how she got her nickname LaLa.

Erik was always high and ignored the baby. When he was sick, everything about the kid bugged him. He was irritated with her crying. He would yell at her, but Tito would always step in and take the baby out of sight to safety.

Denise threw a pillow at Tito, "Aye you in Lala land? Go get your little girlfriend a hot, wet towel with soap on it too, devoladas."

Tito and Tina exchanged embarrassed glances when Denise referred to Tina as Tito's little girlfriend. Zoe-LaLa sat next to Tina, who reached over and gave the baby a loveable kiss on the cheek saying,

"Hi mija-hi mamas."

Zoe-LaLa pointed at Tina's knee saying, "Koko, kiss koko."

Tina hugged the baby replying, "Yes mamas, it's a koko and it hurts."

Zoe-Lala kissed her own hand and touched Tina's knee as if her kiss was going to magically heal Tina's knee. Tina could still smell the marijuana in the air. She fanned the air away from the baby.

Tito pushed through the closed but unlocked restroom for a soapy towel. Tito stopped dead in his tracks as he observed his father sitting on the toilet. Erik was slamming heroin and withdrawing an empty syringe from his right arm. That arm had a peacock tattoo on it that was designed to hide all the scar tissue track marks. Erik had an evil smile on his face. He was unaware of his son's presence until Tito spoke, "Oh sorry Pops, I didn't know you were in here, I'm sorry." Erik was in state of euphoria in a nod, feeling the heroin flow through his veins.

He looked up at his son and said, "Aye Tito, what's up? No, no. It's cool, it's cool. Do what you gotta do lil homito, pero do me a parro and light me a frajo before you go alright? The Camels are on the sink."

Erik removed the bandanna from his bicep, releasing the flow of blood. Now he felt the full effect of the head rush and lovely high. He began scratching his nose. He dropped the empty syringe on the floor. Erik floated to cloud nine. A lovely place close to Heaven where a sinning dope fiend was allowed to dwell. In order to get to this dream state, this temporary form of Heaven, Erik had to go through hell first. His favorite saying was, *The Golden Road to Heaven starts in Hell.* He'd mumble that and laugh when no one else did and yell, "Go to hell! All of you go to hell, you assholes!"

Erik was a real joker in his own loaded mind. He was the joke and asshole though. He'd feed his arms heroin before he fed his son food. His drugs and highs came first. Neither His family nor anything else mattered to him. His life revolved around his heroin, his first love. Erik was scandalous. His word was no good in the hood. He was tarnished with a bad reputation. Because his hustle was weak and slow, there were many days he paid with cold sweat and feverish chills, going through withdrawals and feeling as sick as a dog! That's exactly what he was, a sick dog.

In fact, in the Bible, in the Book of Proverbs 26:11 it speaks of men like Erik. The words of wisdom say…*As a dog returns to his vomit, so fools repeat their folly…*

And that was Erik's exact mindset. The heroin represented the vomit, which Erik returned to everyday, is what made him sick. He was just a fiend willing to pay the agony for the ecstasy.

Tito was staring at his pops sitting on the toilet. He was ashamed of him. He thought, *I never want to end up like him, never!*

Erik muttered to his son, "Tito where's my pinche frajo? Where's my Camel you lil joto faggot idiot!"

He reached out and Tito moved towards the sink and lifted up a cigarette for his father. Tito's heart was racing, pumping fear.

Erik yelled, "I'm talking to you idiot! Do you hear me goddamn it! Stupid fucker!"

"Here Pops, be careful you don't burn yourself," Tito said nervously, handing the cigarette to his pops.

Erik snatched it and toked it with his eyes still closed, mumbling as he exhaled smoke through his nostrils. He began scratching his head and chest, opening his low eyes and yelling at Tito. "Aye man! Tell me something Tito. Why you wanna be a fuckin rata ass cop huh? You fuckin puto, pig lover. Piece of shit, fuckin hura! What's wrong with you? No son of mine is gonna be a snitch rat cop pig! Do you hear me ass hole? I'll kill you before I let you be a cop, you lil son of a bitch!" Erik choked on his words as he stuttered and slurred insults at his son.

Tito was scared now, but knew better than to answer his father's dumb questions. He'd learned the hard way not to talk back to him while he was loaded. Any and every answer, no matter the topic, was wrong, wrong, wrong, and Tito had paid with his blood for giving wrong answers in the past. He was stuck between a rock and a hard place because if he ignored his pops he'd get it for that too. So he was damned if he did and damned if he didn't. He didn't feel like playing his father's mind games tonight, so he chose the lesser of the two evils and ignored his pops' stupid questions and insults.

Erik was half-asleep now, still in a nod, mumbling gibberish. He lost his balance and almost fell into the bathtub. Tito quickly reached over, grabbing his father's shoulders, bringing him back upright.

Tito said, "Whoa Pops don't go falling out on me now. Try to keep your balance."

Erik stood up straight, scratching and combing his big walrus looking mustache with his fingers, then pushing Tito away hollered, "Get your fuckin dick beaters off me kid! I know what the hell I'm doing! I take care of you! You don't take care of me!"

Tito mumbled, "You coulda fooled me."

Erik heard him and half-heartedly swung at his son. "You

ungrateful bastard! What did you say? I'll beat the shit out of ya!"

Tito took a step back, cringing, and he began praying in his head to Jesus. He whispered, *"Lord Jesus protect me. Don't let him hurt me. Help him get off drugs. I love him but hate him like this. I know deep down he's got a good heart, because you created him. I don't want my Pops to die of an overdose. Lord Jesus, please help us somehow. Help him change back to when he was a good pops. It's the drugs Lord. We deserve some happiness and peace don't we? In your precious name, Jesus pour your healing blood on my father."*

Erik's eyes were glossy bloodshot red. He tried to focus on Tito. He was too loaded. This was his third shot of the day.

Zoe-LaLa was crawling towards the restroom to be nosy.

Tito tried cleaning up a little because he didn't want the baby accidentally being poked. He reached down, picked up an empty syringe, and then noticed that there was a second syringe of heroin on the rim of the bathtub. It was a demon-black shade of liquid, filled to 1cc.He placed the empty rig next to the full one then had a sudden thought. Maybe an angel whispering in his ear, *'Empty the full syringe in the sink.'* He was scared though, and not that brave. But his bad dad was so high he might not remember. On second thought, he decided against it. Of course his pops would remember. Heroin was his life. Evidently, Erik planned to do back-to-back shots tonight. They were all set up and ready for his dope binge.

Erik stretched his legs and knees, pushing the syringes into the bathtub. Tito reached into the tub to put the rigs up high, out of the baby's reach. Erik opened his eyes and swore he saw his son's sticky fingers on his last fix. All of a sudden, at the speed of light he flashed on Tito cold cocking Tito in the temple full force. As if he was sober, Erik stood up quickly following up with a one-two combo to Tito's mouth, knocking his front teeth out.

Tito tasted the blood as he flew head first into the tub, letting out a hurtful scream. Tito was dazed, stunned and terrified. His ears were ringing and buzzing and he found himself falling into an agonizing world of pain. He was lost and confused. Discombobulated, choking on his own blood.

Erik had made a leather braided belt in prison, and was now taking it off, wetting it in toilet water. When Tito looked up, he felt the wet welt slap across his burning face, across his shoulder. Tito tried lifting his hands up somewhat to protect himself, but it was apparent that he had lost all control of his body parts. His mind was giving the orders but his body wasn't responding. He felt weak and drained. Then a warm liquid flowed through the front of his pants as he peed on himself.

Erik was in a demon-possessed type of rage whipping his son. Tito had taken beatings before, but this one took the cake. Erik's fist came down hard, crushing his son's jawbones, snapping and breaking them into pieces. Tito was engulfed and overwhelmed with pain.

He heard the baby LaLa crying at the doorway. Her young innocent eyes filled with tears as she saw her brother getting beaten purple and blue. She crawled towards Tito and cried, "Ti Ti, no Ti Ti, Dada bad Dada!"

She knew her dad was being bad and she tried scolding him to leave Ti Ti alone. Ti Ti is what she called Tito.

Erik heard the baby, turned and swung the wet belt at her hollering, "Get the fuck out of here you lil fuckin rug rat before you get it next!"

Baby LaLa trembled in fear, but still tried standing up. Biting her own fist she shouted, "No Dada! No, no!"

Erik cold-heartedly kicked the baby on her arm and she flew into the hallway, crying. Denise ran to the baby's aid. Tito dug deep for strength and found some heart. He reached behind his head and pulled the water nozzle, which was already hanging half way off. Beating Tito was one thing, but beating his baby sister was another and Tito wasn't having it, so he did something of a sacrificial act so that Erik refocused the whipping on him. He threw the metal object at the back of his father's head and got lucky, cracking him dead on, dazing him.

Tito half-consciously gave out a low howl, "Leave my sister alone! I'll kill you! Leave her alone. I swear I'll kill you!" He threatened his father.

Erik felt blood on the back of his head. Still a bit dizzy, he slammed the door shut and locked it.

Denise was screaming on the other side, "Erik please stop! Leave him alone. Please open the door, don't do this!" But Erik ignored his wife.

Erik reached down; picking up the water nozzle and with full force threw it back at Tito, hitting him dead on in the eye. They both yelled as Tito's eye split open, gushing blood on contact. Nevertheless, Tito smiled knowing his plan to protect his baby sister had worked. But now he'd pay the price in pain and blood as a human sacrifice.

What gave him strength was that his Lord and savior Jesus Christ had taken a beating worse than this and survived. Tito had Jesus in his heart and he knew, *Greater is He (Jesus) who is in me than he who is in the world.* He tried desperately to focus and block out the pain, but the pain just kept coming back in agonizing waves as Erik pounded away on Tito. The leather belt tore away at his flesh. Tito imagined Jesus being whipped by the guards, going through a similar situation.

Erik yelled, "Oh you fucked up now you lil bastard. You're gonna wish you were dead by the time I'm done with you!"

Tito believed every word too, because he already wished he were dead, or at least asleep.

Tito could hear Denise cursing and kicking the door. "You better fuckin stop Erik. You asshole, I'm gonna call the cops! Leave him alone, damn it. Stop already!"

Tina picked up LaLa and went outside. She thought about what he was going through and started crying, feeling his pain. He didn't deserve this beating. Tito was a good kid.

Erik was yelling and spitting in Tito's face. "How do you like that muthafucka huh?"

Erik licked the blood off his fingers and then touched the back of his head again. He grew even angrier, shoving his bloody fingers in Tito's mouth yelling, "Here muthafuckin pig, taste this blood!"

Tito was almost unconscious when felt the cherry from his dad's cigarette burn through his face and nose. Tito awoke suddenly and spit blood onto the cigarette, putting the fire out. This aggravated Erik, so he busted out a miniature torch lighter and burned Tito's hands. Tito screamed in agonizing pain as his flesh burned and boiled up! He felt like he was melting and being cooked alive at the same time. A foul odor of burnt flesh is the only thing that saved Tito because Erik became nauseous with the smell and stopped.

He yelled, "See how you smell you rotten son of a bitch. You make me gag!" Erik choked saying, "I know you were trying to steal my Negra you lil fucker. You want heroin huh? I'll give you heroin!"

Tito mumbled, trying to get out of the bathtub.

Erik slugged him in the forehead. "Lay your bitchass down you pig! I thought you wanted to be a cop Tito. Why you tryna steal my dope? Cops don't steal! So you wanna get high now, is that it?"

"No Pops, no! I didn't want you or LaLa to step on the needles, I swear I just…"

SMACK! Tito didn't get to finish his sentence. Erik slapped him across the mouth yelling, "You liar! You lie to me. I know you wanna get high. It's okay, you'll be like me. Like father, like son."

Erik reached around the tub and floor, found the full syringe and smiled, showing it to his son. "Time to face your demons son. I'm gonna give you your first fix, your first shot."

Tito felt sick to his stomach and was dizzy. As he sat soaked in a pool of blood he started flashing back to when he had stood up for Alex because Lil Assassin had stolen his bike. Tito had gotten pistol whipped and knocked out that night. How he felt then was how he felt now. He was close to sleep.

Erik woke Tito up slapping his arm bicep, looking for a vein in Tito's arm. Tito realized the leather belt was wrapped around his arm, stopping the blood flow, just like he'd seen his dad doing to himself so many times. Tito couldn't believe his own father was doing this to him. He tried moving away.

Erik yelled, "Don't move cabron! The needle will break in your arm and go straight into your heart, killing you!"

Tito prayed to God for help and thought, *I can't believe my Pops is dragging me into this nightmare of a hellish world.* Tito felt the needle and he opened his puffy purple eyes. He saw his Pops eyes, bloodshot red. Demon possessed eyes, full of hate, glaring into and piercing Tito's helpless soul. This wasn't his father anymore.

Tito's virgin veins were popped with heroin, the King's White Horse. He yelled as loud as he could, "Noooo Pops pleeaaasssse, heeelp me mooommm…heeelllp meee! I'm sorry Pops, I'm sorry!"

Denise felt chills run through her body when Tito screamed. She kicked the door then ran to the kitchen for a knife to pop open the door and stab Erik to make him stop hurting her son. Poor Tito plead for his life. It was useless though.

Denise desperately tried to break in the door, screaming, "Leave him alone you bastard!"

Erik wickedly laughed and hollered, "Kickback bitch. We're getting high now so relax!"

Tito felt the heroin rush to his heart and brain. He gasped for air mumbling, "Oh my God, Jesus help me!"

Tito's pain surprisingly started to decrease. Erik slammed half of the contents of the syringe into Tito's arm and pulled it out saying, "You like that boy? Jesus ain't got nuttin to do with it. Ain't no Jesus or no police gonna help or save you. King Heroin is your savior now!"

Tito was looking into the devil's face when he stared at his father. For some reason Tito started to relax and feel better. You can even go as far as to say that he even felt *good*, but drained of energy. Tito had no more fight in him. He didn't care about living. He just closed his eyes and enjoyed the high, falling into a dream state. Hearing his father's haunting laugh, he embraced death.

Death felt good to Tito. He felt chills and little electric tingles flowing through his battered body. No more pain. Something beautiful was overriding the excruciating pain. Tito felt joy, love and happiness. He kind of even forgot what he was going through. Emotions stirred in him, feelings he'd never felt all at once. His spirit was telling him that something was wrong, but everything felt lovely and all right. This love he felt wasn't true love. It wasn't God's love, but it was an illusion of peace and love. Tito had no personal feeling of the terror that would follow. Tito now knew why his father chased the dragon, why he chased the dope. Tito thought, *Pops finally killed me.I'm in heaven.* Tito was delirious. He had no idea he was still alive and as loaded as a gun. Tito heard his father's voice. Tito knew his father wouldn't be allowed into heaven, so he wondered if maybe he was in hell.

As if on cue, Erik said, "Feels good huh son? Welcome to Hell on earth."

Tito opened his eyes and saw his Pops sliding the needle into his own arm again, finishing off the other 50cc's of heroin.

"Now it's my turn, I'll meet you in Dragon Paradise son." He smiled and then grunted, falling sideways towards the sink, stumbling into the full-length mirror. Shattered glass particles flew everywhere.

"Whoa! Fuck ese, I think I did a lil too much." Erik reached for the door handle. "Help me Denise," he stammered. Erik grabbed at his chest as he fell to the floor. "I can't breathe, son of a bitch!"

He gasped for air and then began the flopping fish-out-of-water routine. The devil frowned and God smiled.

Tito opened his eyes and saw his father getting a taste of his own medicine. He laughed and muttered, "Go to hell Pops, die, die and burn in the pits you devil. I hate you, I hope you die."

Tito was full of mixed emotions; he loved his father but hated what he had done to him. Tito cried like a baby. He floated to unknown dimensions so high that he thought he was flying, so he stretched out his arms, which somehow seemed to have turned into wings. Just then, his body began to spasm and mimic his fathers'. They were both overdosing on heroin. The poisonous venom was killing them both. Two birds with one stone.

Denise usually turned a blind eye to Erik's disciplining of Tito, but she had a gut feeling that he'd definitely gone overboard this time. Her heart raced and pumped fear when silence came in the restroom. Denise knew her son was dying on the other side of that door. She usually didn't mind when Erik got high because he was all lovey dovey with her. He was more tolerable, easier to live with. When Erik was sick or fiending for a fix, he was grouchy, violent and irritated at everyone and everything.

She'd give him some of her welfare check to get high. Then she'd go to Rialto, to St. Catherine's Church and get free food that they'd give out to the poor. Erik beat her purple and blue for not giving him money, so she learned to give him some. But she'd buy the kids food first. They traveled by bus everywhere. Denise would always be invited to church, but she declined politely because she didn't believe in God. Her thoughts were' *'If there was a God, she didn't want anything to do with him because he allowed so much evil in the world to happen.'*

The people at church would tell her, "God doesn't do the evil, the devil does. Take the "d" off devil, and you've got evil. God does stop evil, but everything happens for a reason. We are made in God's image. He is blessing you with food and clothes for your kids. Blame the devil, not God for the evil in this world. The devil is the father of lies and deception. He wants you to hate God. Try praying mija."

Denise was in a panicked frenzy, kicking the door and trying to pop the lock with a knife.

The neighbor, Redrum, ran into the apartment and asked, "What's going on?"

"Erik's trippin again!" screamed Tina. "He's killing Tito, help me open the door." sobbed Denise.

Redrum pulled out his pistol and pushed Denise away from the door. "Move, I've got this," he ordered. Then he shot the lock off the door and kicked it open. "Oh fuck! What the fuck happened!" Rum shouted as he surveyed the bloody scene.

Denise ran into the room past Rum. Her guttural, anguished cry echoed through the apartment when she saw Erik sprawled out on the floor and she rushed over to Tito.

"Oh mijo!" she cried, "please mijo say something, don't die! Help me Rum, help me get him outta the tub!" she begged as she desperately tried to pull him out of the tub.

Redrum did just that. He picked Tito up and carried him to the couch in the living room, laying him down carefully.

Tina ran into the living room crying, "I called the cops and ambulance. They're on the way!"

The sirens were already getting closer. Baby LaLa cried at the sight of Tito. Denise had grabbed a wet towel and some ice cubes and she began wiping away the blood as she knelt on the floor next to him. She looked at his swollen purple body and she froze with fear. Denise knew Erik was dying, and examining Tito's beat up, swollen purple body, she knew that Tito was dying too. She knew CPR and knew how to bring him back from an overdose, since she had done it several times before. This wasn't her first picnic in the park. She needed the ice to put on his nuts, but there was only enough ice for one person. Tito wasn't moving, but Erik was. She could hear him thrashing around in the restroom. She could not believe that was Tito lying there lifelessly, beaten to a pulp. She froze with fear, overridden with guilt, jaw open, crying, hands over her broken heart, trying to keep it from falling into pieces. She felt pulled in two directions. The question was-whom should she save, Erik or Tito? Her life flashed before her eyes and she dropped the ice cubes and towel to the floor. She was in shock. She was of no help to her son, who had already stopped breathing.

Luckily for Tito, the ambulance finally arrived. But it was a little too late for Erik. As the ambulance raced, containing poor Tito's limp, dying body to the County Hospital, the Coroner's office hauled the scumbag Erik away in a body bag.

That cold night Denise lost both Erik and Tito to a drug overdose. Heroin took both her loves and this was something she would have to live with for the rest of her life. You see, Erik died of an overdose, which was exactly what he deserved. Tito lived, but Denise lost Tito to heroin. Tito's hopes and childhood dreams of living a straight life as a cop died that night too. The innocent Tito she knew died. He was no longer that kid. Never in a million years would anyone have ever thought that Tito would become a heroin addict. And one of the luckiest, slickest, slyest and sneakiest ones at that.

Overnight Tito became a slave to the King's White Horse, all the while still keeping some morals and a golden heart.

But it's been said, Beware *of the King's White Horse, for if you ride him, he'll drag you to the pits of hell and then buck you off to burn in the flames forever.*

One who hears but does not listen, pass them by. They'll be dead in their misery and death will overtake their spirits and souls.

Like father, like son-

But not by Tito's choice. Not by his choice at all. Enjoy the ride on the King's White Horse and try to catch the snakes and dragons we are chasing along the way.

GAME TIME
PRESENT DAY 2008
TWENTY-FOUR YEARS LATER

It was May fifth, 5:45 a.m. and the morning was crisp and chilly. The Colton Police Department Drug Task Force team was patiently awaiting orders. They were parked behind the Colton Sun Market in three black unmarked vans with mirror-tinted windows. The twelve-man SWAT team, a.k.a. the 'dirty dozen', looked like ninjas. They wore black fatigues, black boots, black bulletproof vests, kneepads, black bulletproof helmets and face shields. They all carried high-powered weapons with infrared beams attached at the barrel. The back of their uniforms glowed yellow reading *SWAT* and *POLICE*. Three undercover officers wore black ski masks so as not to blow their cover when the raid went down. Then they'd be able to go straight to the stash spots. Surveillance was set up.

Sergeant Garza had his night vision binoculars pointed at the yellow two-story house on the corner of Mt.Vernon and G Street. Sgt. Garza ordered into his radio, "Lewis, it's time. Move to the eastern entrance of the alley."

Officer Lewis replied, "Yes Sir Sarge. We're on our way." He then tapped his driver's shoulder and the van crept to secure the perimeter with the four-man squad.

Sgt. Garza again ordered into his radio, "Second squad, you know what to do, it's a green light Williams."

Officer Williams responded, "Roger that sir" and his van slowly drove through the quiet neighborhood. There was still fifteen minutes or so until sunrise. The raid had to go down quickly and perfectly. The officers still blended in with the shadows of the night for two crucial reasons. Number one, the SWAT team wanted to capture and keep the element of surprise on their side to lessen the chances of casualties to their team and number two, the children would start exiting their homes heading to school within the hour and CPD didn't want any innocent kids being caught in crossfire.

Sgt. Garza cocked back his death black A-P-9 millimeter, sliding a golden hollow point bullet into the cold but soon-to-be hot chamber. He adjusted his night vision binoculars. He focused on a tall six foot tall skinny Mexican in his mid-thirties lurking around the area. The suspect was wearing a navy and baby blue North Carolina baseball cap and matching jersey. This was North Colton gangsters color and gear. He tightened up his belt, snugging the black khakis as he headed straight to Redrum's dope house. Two brown pit bulls were running along the fence barking at the suspect. He kicked at the fence, flicking a lit cigarette in their faces as he growled back and provoked the mutts. A rooster crowed in the distance. He looked around suspiciously, then strolled up to the drug connection's house and knocked.

Sgt. Garza handed the binoculars off to his female partner, who was sitting shotgun. "Berry, is that Tito 'Lucky' Lopez knocking on the dope man's door?"

Officer Berry scratched her nose and took a look answering, "Yes sir, it sure is Sarge and he's playing with fire, about to get burned. Ol' Tito has two strikes hanging over his head. I'll bet twenty dollars he has drug paraphernalia, stolen goods, or maybe even a gun in his possession. That will get him his third strike. Swing and a miss-any takers?"

Officer Morgan in the backseat replied, "I've booked Tito on two felonies alone just this year and his lucky ass always seems to beat the cases. He just finished a ninety-day dry out parole violation in Chino. I'll take that bet but may I add that the case has to stick in order for you to collect, and I'll bet another twenty dollars that he's already strung out."

Officer Berry reached back and shook on the bet. "That's a bet. We'll probably break even. We're about to bust his little bubble and take his morning fix away."

Officer Morgan said, "Yeah, don't feel bad, and when you lose the bet don't feel bad, Officer Yang and Lara have lost more than three cases against Tito. Lara's got a hard on for him. He hates him with a passion. Tito put paperwork on Yang and Lara complaining of police brutality and planting evidence. Internal affairs cleared Yang and Lara for now, and Tito was cut loose on five strikes so as not to pursue a lawsuit. Lucky motherfucker! Yang and Lara would love to be involved in this raid if they knew he was here."

Sgt. Garza rolled down his window half way for some fresh air and said, "I-uh- might have cleared Yang and Lara for that single incident, but there's still an ongoing investigation for prior suspicious unprofessional conduct. I know they're corrupt, but we just have to prove it. I saw Tito when they worked him over with flashlight therapy, cracking his skull open. He could have been a rich man, but he backed off and stayed in the hospital for three weeks, high on morphine pills and injections. That's all he cared about."

"Tito's in the house. The thing about Tito is he's basically harmless to others. He's not violent; he's just killing himself slowly, slamming that junk. The most violent thing he's got under his jacket is that he did an armed robbery a few years back. The weapon was a syringe full of blood. He told the Circle 'K' clerk that it was AIDS infected blood and to hand over the loot or he'd stick her with it," said Officer Berry. They all laughed.

Sgt. Garza tapped the steering wheel, "Yeah, I remember that case. That was his first strike and we tested the blood. It was clean. Man the things dope fiends think of."

Officer Saens from the back seat said, "What about when Lara and Yang arrested Tito at Cesar Chavez Park? Tito and Sharky were in a stolen car, slamming heroin. Tito was in a nod, Sharky was poking himself when Lara crept up on the driver's side window, pistol drawn. Lara told me that he saw Sharky throw his weapon in Tito's lap while he was nodding out. Yet in his reports he never mentioned that the gun was really Sharky's. They broke that party up! Talk about a rude awakening. Yang broke the window with his baton, putting his gloc in Tito's face. Tito got lucky then too. He pled out to possession of a weapon, possession of stolen property and driving a car without the owner's consent instead of carjacking. Sharky did the carjacking. We knew it but couldn't prove it. That was Tito's second strike."

Sgt. Garza turned on the ignition and put the van in drive. Speaking into his radio, he said, "It's game time boys, let's rock n roll!"

He drove towards Redrum's dope house as Officer Berry cocked her gun back saying, "Let's see if Tito catches strike number three. Is today your lucky day Tito, or has your luck finally run out?" The van peeled out, tires burning rubber as they sped down Mt. Vernon Avenue.

RIDING THE BENCH
PAST-1984

Denise Lopez lost her whole life and freedom with one shot after Erik and Tito overdosed. As the CPD investigated, all the Lopez's family secrets seemed to be coming to light. Denise was in the county jail fighting a string of felony charges-child neglect, kidnapping of baby Zoe and possession of drugs and paraphernalia. Both Tito and Zoe had been placed into foster care. They were living a couple cities away from Colton in the city of Highland with a white couple named Bill and Hope. The couple had two boys of their own, ages six and eight years old. They seemed to be withdrawn. They hardly spoke to Tito or Zoe. Tito felt that the only reason that Bob and Hope took in foster children was for the checks. Tito wasn't comfortable there and didn't trust his foster parents, but he stayed and behaved because he knew it was temporary, just until his mother was released from jail. What bothered him was that he hadn't heard from his mother in over two months. He was worried. He'd written to her over ten times with no response.

Tito shared a bed with Zoe-LaLa. One night he woke up because he heard his baby sister crying. She wasn't in the bed so he crept down the hall to find her. What he saw in the living room blew his mind and scared him at the same time. Bob and Zoe were both naked sitting on the couch. Child porn was on the TV and it was dark but Tito could see Bob touching Zoe, trying to get her to kiss his private parts. Zoe kept pushing and struggling to get away from Bob the sick molester. She cried for Tito.

"Ti Ti! Ti Ti!"

Tito's heart pumped rage as anger engulfed him, but he had to think fast and then act even faster. He looked towards the locked front door, crawled over to it and quietly began to unlock the latches. He opened the door slowly and then crept into the kitchen and got the biggest and sharpest butcher knife he could find. He took ten deep breaths to slow down his racing heart and calm his nerves. He was shaking with fear but he had to overcome that fear and be brave for Zoe. He made a vow to always help her no matter what.

Tito was crawling on the carpet behind the couch when he heard a door open down the hall and heard Hope's voice saying, "Bob are you still awake sweetheart?"

As she got closer to him, Tito saw Hope fixing her robe and wiping the sleep out of her eyes. Tito was hidden in the dark, but felt relieved that he wouldn't have to stab Bob after all because Hope would stop the pervert from hurting his sister.Tito couldn't believe what he saw and heard next. He was hoping it was all just a nightmare and that he'd wake up at any moment when he heard Hope say, "Next time you're going to have fun, invite your wifey."

Hope then slipped off her nightgown until she was also naked. Hope picked up Zoe and gave Bob a French kiss. Tito's mind snapped instantly. With quickness, he jumped up from behind the couch, swinging the knife as hard as he could.

The cold steel sliced through Bob's Adam's apple, in and out of his throat. Bob's eyes bulged out of his eye sockets. Hope backed up terrified, dropping Zoe to the floor as she cried and crawled away. Bob instinctively grabbed his bloody throat, trying to scream in pain but no sounds came out. Tito kept stabbing a frozen in shock, perverted Bob. He stabbed him in his eye, his cheeks, head, arms, hands and chest. Hope screamed at the top of her lungs, "Stop! Stop! I'm calling the police, stop it now!" as she backpedaled and fumbled towards the telephone. Zoe was crying hysterically and Bob fell to the floor next to her. He reached in her direction and Tito mounted Bob and began stabbing away like a deranged lunatic. He had lost it. He was almost demon possessed you can say. He couldn't believe he was doing it, but something in him made him keep stabbing. *The devil made me do it' he thought, or better yet, God made me stab these devils that were molesting God's little angel Zoe.* Tito was thrown off Bob as he tried crawling away. He was weak though and riddled with puncture wounds.

Tito was still in his deadly trance state-of-mind. He wacked Bob's asshole and testicles. He stabbed at Bob's penis. More blood gushed and oozed. This molester was getting exactly what all child molesters deserved to get. Tito ran at Hope and stabbed her in the face and stomach. She managed to run into the restroom screaming and crying and locked the door. Tito saw Bob was slumped over, not moving, possibly dead. Maybe he was even playing opossum. Zoe was crying, pulling Tito's pants leg, which brought him back to reality. Tito couldn't believe the scene before his eyes; let alone the fact that *he'd* done all of it. It was as if a demon had taken over his body and had him kill some shit off, leaving Tito to suffer the consequences and clean up the mess. Tito knew this was wrong, but he thought he'd done wrong for the right reason. He had to protect his baby sister Zoe-LaLa. His clothes were full of blood and so was the baby from crawling in it.

Tito picked up his sister and gave her a hug and a kiss. She shivered and he covered her with a blanket and yelled at Hope, "I'm calling the police bitch-if you come out I'll stab the shit out of you and kill you!"

He then pulled the phone out of the wall and ran out of the front door, holding the baby. He ran barefooted through the cold night as fast as he could, looking back as shadows reached out for him. Tito and Zoe finally made it to the Arco gas station about a mile away. There He called his girlfriend Tina's house. She answered and accepted the collect call. The first thing he said was, "We need help!"

Tina snuck out of her apartment and ran to the group of Colton gangsters that were still out late night partying in the parking lot of the Rose Garden Apartments. The aroma of weed and sherm was in the air. Redrum's black El Camino was bumping Spice 1 tunes out the low-low. Tina whispered in Redrum's ear, telling him what just happened to Tito and Zoe-LaLa. She begged, "They need help! Can you go pick them up Rum? Please? I don't want Tito to go to juvenile hall!"

Redrum flicked his cigarette butt into the air and told his homeboys, "Aye homies, looks like Little Tito and baby Zoe need us. They fell into the clutches of a piece of shit. Time to clean house. Bring yo straps, it's time to peel some wigs back, let's bounce."

A murder squad of ten gangsters mobbed up in three lowriders swooped in to pick up Tito and Zoe. They found Tito and Zoe at the Arco gas station, shivering and scared. Tito laced Redrum on what exactly had happened, which made Redrum flaming hot. He gave his jacket to Tito and pulled a pancho out from his back seat to wrap Zoe up in. He gave Travieso some money to go buy them some food and take them back to Rum Rum's apartment. The other two lowriders were on a mission to clean up little Tito's mess. They drove up to the scene and crept back to Bob and Hope's house to finish the job. To do, if necessary, exactly what needed to be done.

Bob was half-dead, still wheezing and starving for air. Rum Rum picked up Tito's knife and reached for Bob's penis. He sliced it off and put it in Bob's mouth, kicking him in the face just to humiliate him before he killed him. He then slowly stuck the butcher knife in Bob's ass hole twisting and slicing his guts. Buddha and Flaco dragged Hope out of the restroom by her hair.

She was on her knees begging, "Please don't hurt me, I didn't do anything!"

"That's right bitch," said Flaco, "you didn't do nothin to stop that piece of shit husband of yours from molesting Zoe, so for that, you die!"

Buddha put the revolver to her temple as Rum Rum grabbed Bob by his hair and said, "Look at your bitch die cuz of you!"

A defeated Bob yelled, "No!" as Buddha pulled the trigger and smoked Hope.

Rum Rum smiled wickedly whispering, "Your turn!"

He pulled out his pistol and shot Bob in his dick, well, where his dick *used* to be. Then in his throat and finally in Bob's heart and face until there were no more bullets left. Redrum pocketed the knife just as Bob and Hope's two boys came out of their bedrooms. Redrum, Buddha and Flaco drew down on the youngsters. Their eyes teared up at the site of their slaughtered parents. Redrum put his finger to his mouth and said, "Shhh, this is just a bad dream, go back to sleep boys, go to your room."

Then the wrecking crew split before the cops got there, leaving little to no evidence other than the bodies.

The next few days were rough on Tito and Zoe. Once Tito got back to the Rose Garden Apartments, he broke into his old apartment and him and baby Zoe-LaLa made the apartment their own. Redrum paid off the landlord, giving him a half-ounce of speed to allow Tito and Zoe to live in their old apartment and not say anything to the cops or Child Protective Services (CPS). The G's from North Colton were officially looking out for Tito and Zoe now. The gangsters respected little Tito for whacking the child molester Bob. He'd protected his baby sister by any means necessary, as they do in the hood.

The only thing was that the hood was hella hot now. CPD patrolled the complex all week, more than usual, looking for Tito and Zoe, which slowed down drug business a little. CPD kept coming up empty until two weeks after the double homicide in Highland. That day, Tito was cooking some eggs and Top Ramen soup for baby Zoe-LaLa. Tina was also there at the apartment with them playing with the baby. The ice cream man was making his rounds in the complex, music blaring.

When Zoe-LaLa heard the music, she said excitedly, "Ice keem Ti Ti, ice keem."

Tito reached in his pockets and pulled off a five-dollar bill from a fat wad of money. He had managed to hustle up two-hundred and thirty dollars by doing things for the G's in the complex. Tito gave Tina the five dollars.

"Do you want anything?" she asked as she picked up the baby and walked outside.

"Yeah, a popcorn and a strawberry shortcake," Tito answered.

He decided to go outside to and watch over his sister and girlfriend from the yard. A four-year-old little kid named Chico raced up to Tito on his Big Wheel. He was going so fast that Tito had to jump over Lil Chico who skidded to a halt in front of him.

"Did you see that Tito, did you see how fast I was going? Cant no one go faster than me huh Tito?"

Tito laughed, "Yes sir, you're the fastest Lil Chico, you're the champ ma boy. Can't no one beat you. You're the next little Nascar champion if you ask me!"

Lil Chico pushed towards Tito and asked him, "What's my prize then? Can it be an ice cream, or two Chico Sticks? That's my favorite, Yeah, or saladitos better."

Tito pulled another five-dollar bill out and knelt down next to Lil Chico, rubbing his hair and messing it up. Tito told Chico, "Your prize is five dollars. Go buy whatever you want champ."

Lil Chico saw Tito's wad of money and said, "Wow man are you a baller Tito? I can buy all that, everything I want? I'm gone!" And with that, Lil Chico peeled out towards the ice cream man.

Tito went back inside the apartment and got Zoe's food together. He chopped up the boiled eggs and fried hot dogs then put it on the top of the warm Top Ramen noodles. This was the baby's favorite meal, and it was cheap. He was praying over the food when suddenly four Colton cops running into his pad rudely interrupted him. He heard the whistle alerting him, but it was too late. The ice cream man had distracted everyone. Tito was caught slipping off guard and was arrested on the spot. He was cuffed and put into the back of the cop car. Everybody in the Rose Garden Apartments gathered around to see what was going on.

The gangsters were in the cuts of the shadows, laying low out of sight, yet they were eyeing the police. A couple of cops were searching

Tito's apartment, looking for Zoe and evidence.

One officer sat in the driver's seat of the car asking Tito questions like, "What happened to your foster parents? Why did you kill them? Where's Zoe?"

Tito was looking out the back window of the car, ignoring the pig's questions.

The cop just kept asking him more questions though. He asked, "Who was with you son? Where is the gun? Was Mr. Blanch molesting you and Zoe? We found child porn in his house. He was a sick bastard and got what he had coming if you ask me." The pig tried using reverse-psychology telling Tito, "You did right Tito. Just tell me where the gun is so I can make sure no one finds it and you won't do no real time son. I got your back."

Tito looked him in the eyes through the rear view mirror and could easily tell that the pig was lying, trying to gather Intel. Tito smirked and then looked into the crowd for Tina and Zoe. He spotted them far off and watched them sneak into Lil Eddie's apartment unseen.

Tito then spotted Redrum about forty-five yards away hiding behind a tree. He and Tito made eye contact and Redrum put his pointer finger to his lips motioning, 'Shhh', for Tito to stay quiet. Tito understood and nodded back, 'yes, ok'. Redrum said something in Speedy's ear and then Speedy sprinted off with a purpose. Redrum then waved Lil Chico on over and said something to the kid and handed him some money. A plan was now in motion to help Tito out. A minute or two later, several gunshots rang out in the back of the apartments. Speedy was shooting in the air creating a diversion. He then ran up and dumped the gun right in front of the cop car that Tito and the cop were sitting in.

When the cop saw this, he jumped out of the car, yelling into his CB, "Officer needs assistance, shots fired! Shots fired!"

The cop started chasing Speedy, abandoning his cop car. The other two cops on the scene searching Tito's apartment also gave chase, hot on Speedy's trail hollering, "Get down, get down or I'll shoot!"

Guns in hand, CPD ran in the direction they'd seen Speedy go, but Speedy had decided to shake the pigs and stop playing games with them. Little did they know Speedy was a track star in Jr. High before he started gang banging. He left them three little piggies in the dust, hitting fences left and right. Mission complete. They didn't call him Speedy for nothing.

Lil Chico was doing his job too. He rode his Big Wheel up to the cop cars' back door and opened it from the outside. After all, no cop would ever arrest a four-year old for helping someone escape because they did not know better. Tito jumped out of the cop car, still cuffed. Redrum and Dreamer swooped up in a blue Racer Civic with tinted windows with the back door open and Tito dove in.

Redrum said, "We're gone lil homie, we got you. Don't even trip." They smashed out of the complex like they were in the Indie 500. They got ghost, disappearing real quick.

Tito asked, "What about LaLa? I need to get my sister out of there."

"Don't trip lil homie. My hinas got LaLa. She's taken care of. We gotta get you to the hideout. We're slidin to the eastside. The homie Listo gots a lay low chill spot. Zoe will be there in a while, soon as the PoPo roll out the hood," Redrum told him.

The Civic was weaving in and out of alleys, heading towards the Hannah Street hideout. Tito was sweating up a storm, still cuffed, moving around on the backseat. He felt lucky to have a homie, even a friend like Redrum who'd help him escape the cops and even kill those no good people that had hurt his family. He felt a new respect for Redrum.

As if he'd read Tito's mind Rum said, "We'll get the cuffs off at Listo's pad, lil homie. What was that pig saying in the car?"

Tito shifted and said, "The pig was asking about my foster parents. They were both killed. I think I killed them both."

Dreamer, who was driving the ride, laughed saying, "The lil homie put down two 187's, not bad for his first hit que no?"

Redrum looked back at Tito and told him, "Just so you know, both them pieces of shit were still alive when I rolled up…so don't let your conscience fuck you up. You did a cold number on them cats, but they were alive. That's all you gotta know. Best not to wake sleeping dogs. What did you tell the pigs?"

"Nothing, cuz I don't know nothing," Tito answered.

Redrum smiled saying, "Yeah man, that's what's up. I got your back lil homie. Keep it gangsta. You got me, I got you. You'll be all right soon enough. We gotta figure a way outta this mess. Tito, you're the luckiest dude I know. You always get caught up in some madness, but luck comes around and gets you outta trouble. You're nickname is Lucky from now on."

Tito smiled and said "Lucky, huh? Yeah I like that. I guess I've had some luck in my life. Why not, fuck it.Lucky it is!"

The streets of Colton were going to be hot for the next few days. Redrum was praying that S.M.A.S.H. gang task force didn't start doing gang sweeps in the hood, looking for baby Zoe and Lucky Tito. He had a lot of money to make and couldn't afford a cheap loss. The thing was that he was starting to look at Tito and Zoe like family, and family came first in his books, so his mission was to hide them both out at all costs.

BATTER UP
PRESENT DAY, MAY 5TH, 2008-6:05 A.M.

Tito was going through withdrawals bad. He was fiending for a fix. He didn't know if he was coming or going as he knocked on the door of the yellow house. He snuck peeks through the dusty windows as goose bump chills riddled through his achy body. He had a fever, his nerves were shot, hands and bones aching, and he had a vicious migraine. He couldn't eat, sleep or shit in peace. He hated life right about then.

Tito could have avoided this sickness if he'd changed hustle tactics. He could have felt well and stayed high if he'd picked up a gun and jacked what he needed. He didn't though. He chose to steal from stores, commit petty theft licks and do odd jobs. He'd work a job to get his fix. As soon as he was done scoring a shot, he was on his way to the Stater Bros. warehouse on La Cadena Drive to wave down diesel truck drivers who were exhausted and in need of help unloading their trucks. Tito usually made sixty to one hundred dollars a day doing this work. He'd also get an eight ball sack of meth upfront and sell it to the truck drivers for one hundred and fifty dollars. He'd make a fifty-dollar profit. The truck drivers lived off Red Bull and methamphetamine.

No one was answering the front door when he knocked at the dope spot, so Tito decided to creep to the side of the pad. He tried opening the side wooden gate. No dice, it was locked. He pulled himself up on the fence to jump over but a loose board gave way, causing Tito to fall face first onto a pile of loose cans. The loud noise incited the two pit bulls who'd already been barking alongside the fence. The two vicious monsters were growling, spitting and scratching at the wooden fence, trying to get under it. They were even biting each other during all the excitement. One of the dogs lived up to his breed name, pit bull, and rammed his head into the boards like a bull, eager to get a bite of Tito. Tito was dizzy from the fall and kicked dirt at the mutts yelling, "Stupid dogs shut the fuck up!"

He was already irritated when he heard an automatic strap cock back. Click clack! A golden bullet slid into the chamber. Tito froze as he saw his dope connect's arm sticking out of the window holding a pistol aimed right at him. The 44 Magnum sent deadly chills through Tito's soul.

Redrum, the dope connect, hollered, "What the fuck you doin Lucky! Kill all that racket fool! You burnin the spot man!"

Tito looked up and made his way carefully away from the scattered cans.

"Chill homie, chill Rum. Put your toy away. I know you aint tryna murder your best customer."

Redrum had one eye closed. There was a 187 tattooed on the eyelid and he squinted at Tito through the open eye with an evil grin across his mug. He had just about put Tito out of his misery. He said, "You're right but you better have that forty bones you owe me. Cash money boy!" he said as he put his gun away.

Tito answered, "I got some merchandise worth more than forty dollaz, don't trip."

He reached in his pocket and pulled out two gold chains. One had a crucifix charm dangling on it. Then he blew the dust and dirt off the gold watch he slid off his wrist.

Tito proudly said, "Watchu know bout this shit, 14k across the board and the watch is a Casio, but it's over a hundred dawg. Will you take this stuff, squash my forty debt and give me four twenty dollar balloons of tar?"

Tito was working his dope fiend hustle, showcasing the jewels as though he worked at a jewelry store. He walked to the window and handed Rum Rum the merchandise.

Redrum examined it and smiled saying, "This shit's kinda flossy Lucky. This'll save me from havin to go shop for my lady. Today's her birthday."

Tito watched through the window as Redrum spanked the ass of his naked girlfriend who was asleep on the bed.

He said, "Aye babe, wacha. Do you like these cadenas or what? If so I'll getem as yo birthday present."

A female voice answered, "Fuck Yeah! This rope's badass. I'm glad you remembered my birthday this time too."

Redrum looked back at Tito saying, "Aye Lucky you got priors for pushin fake shit. I aint gonna be okee doked again. Ima test this shit first and if it's real then I'll squash the forty and give you three balloons, fat twenty dollars of that bomb black heroin. Spera, I'll be back." He disappeared out of sight of the window and Lucky's eyes opened wide with excitement and he licked his lips in anticipation.

Squatting down to pull a syringe out of his socks, he hollered into the window, "Aye Rum let me use your restroom to fix. I gotta get right and then I gotta go to work!"

He heard Redrum yelling from inside the room saying, "If it's legit gold you can, but if you know its wack, you best to get ghost now cuz ima blast yo ass for tryin to pull a fast one."

Lucky adjusted his North Colton hat and strolled to the back door to wait. He had to piss. There was a tree he could piss on close by, but the dogs were still barking. He threw a big boulder at the bottom of the fence in their direction to scare them. The wooden fence cracked some, but Tito paid no attention. He pissed behind the tree and as he was zipping up, he heard a low monstrous growl that scared the shit out of him. It was too close for comfort. Then he felt hot breath and sharp teeth grazing his arm. He quickly pulled away as he screamed, "Oh shit! Aaaauuuuggghhh you muthafuckin mutt!"

He kicked and backpedaled as the brown beast regained ground, kicking up dust, throwing a U-turn. The wild animal charged head down like a raging bull toward Tito. Lucky looked for something high to jump onto. There was an old red knocked over shopping cart within sight. He thought, 'too low, not that.' He sprinted off towards the back yard gate that was open. The hungry little demon wanted Mexican food for breakfast and Lucky wasn't trying to become the main dish. That pit was vicious and had snuck under the fence. Lucky's heart was racing and the pit was close on his tail. He tried to slam the gate in the killer pit's face, but no luck, the gate was stuck. The dog was on his path step for step, teeth gnashing and barking up a storm. Lucky finally made it into the alley, jumped up and pulled himself up onto a six-foot grey brick wall.

He was safe. The bull fell short and was jumping in circles, leaping against the wall, not able to reach his target. What he did get though was Lucky's baseball cap, and he was tearing it to shreds. Lucky was scared out of his wits.

He stood up on the wall cursing at the dog. "Stupid fuckin mutt, I ought to call the dog pound on your ass!"

He spat on the dog and then checked his pierced arm. It was nothing major. Lucky noticed the other pit bull squiggling under the fence where Lucky had thrown the boulder earlier. Lucky felt stupid and thought, *Damn, I'm my own worst enemy. I broke the damn fence.*

Redrum came strolling out the back door looking for his customer and seemed amused that his neighbors' dog was harassing Lucky. He busted up laughing, "Aye Lucks, Ol' Felony gots yo ass pinned up on that wall huh? Ha-ha! I'll tell you what, I got three extra balloons of dope for you if you can make it past Felony and come get em."

Lucky Tito wasn't feeling too lucky so he gave the middle finger to the dope man and yelled, "Up yours fool! I aint here to entertain you. I'll take what you owe me, just call the mutt off."

But Tito being a dope fiend examined the scene and was thinking of a way to take Redrum up on his offer, even if he had to flirt with death or play the clown roll. His addiction would be the death of him. He decided against it when he saw Redrum slap his knee and whistle for the dog.

"Felony, come on boy! Come on, I gotta shot gun blast of chronic for you boy come on!" he called to the beast.

Felony's half tail wagged with excitement when he heard the word chronic, and if Lucky didn't know better, he thought he actually saw the stoner pit bull crack a smile as he raced off to Redrum's side. The dope man took a deep breath of chronic and kneeled down petting Felony. He then opened the dog's mouth and blew a big cloud of smoke into the dogs' mouth. The dog chewed at the smoke getting a shotgun high. Redrum smacked the pit on the nose then began wrestling with it. Along came the second pit bull, Cyclona, sniffing at the scent of the strong potent herb. She had to follow suit and Redrum repeated the 'getting the dogs high' ritual.

Felony barked, spooked at something in the front yard. All of a sudden there was a loud boom! It sounded like a grenade blowing up in front of the house. Then the sound of glass breaking and screams followed by rapid gunfire was heard. Boom! Boom! Boom! Pop, Pop, Pop!

Redrum was instantly alert. He pulled out his 44 Magnum and slapped the dog on the ass hollering, "Get em Cyclona, get em Felony! Sickem boy, kill em!" Felony ran into the house and Redrum was hot on his tracks, gun out, ready to kill at will. His first thought was that some enemies were trying to do a home invasion and rob him. The pit Cyclona ran to the side of the house ready to attack.

Lucky Tito was still in the alley standing on the six-foot wall and saw the chaos unravel before his dilated eyes. Three individuals, all in black, wearing ski masks were creeping alongside the yellow house, assault rifles raised. Cyclona saw them before they saw her and that was their first mistake. In an instant she was on them. She refocused on one of their legs and grip-locked her jaw on it, swinging back and forth trying to rip it out of the man's knee sockets something vicious. He screamed in pain.

At first, Lucky had the same thought Rum Rum had. These were jackers on a mission. But then Lucky noticed the yellow glowing letters on the invaders' chest. They read, POLICE and then he noticed that they were all wearing bulletproof vests with SWAT on the back. Then he heard more shots, Pop! Pop! Pop! Boom! Boom! Boom! He heard an automatic fire spray, Rararara. He saw shock grenades and smoke bombs being thrown into the house.

The upper story windows were being broken out from the inside. Two gangsters jumped out onto the roof. One was dressed in all black, wearing a jersey with white letters that read *EAST SIDES DEADLIEST*. Lucky recognized his homeboy Trooper from East Colton, Hanna St. He was holding a 12 gauge Mossberg. He was pumping it, blasting into the crowd of cops below. He recognized the other gangster too. He was Dreamer from the north side. He was running along the roof, tryin to get over to the neighbor's first story house. He needed to get free or die trying. The shit was that serious.

The cops below were trying to help the cop that was being chewed up by Cyclona. He was screaming, Get em off me! Get this bitch off me. Shoot em! One cop pulled out his revolver and tried to get a clear shot while the other cops beat Cyclona with sticks and rifles. There was too much movement for a clear shot. At the same time as if to add insult to injury, Trooper got the pigs in his sight and started blasting the 12 Shots.

One officer blasted back and another took a knee and covered the back door a second too late, because right then and there Redrum came running out and jumped the five steps landing right on top of the cop. They both began fighting and wrestling.

"Get the fuck off me pig, I'll kill you bitch, get the fuck off!" shouted Rum as he reached for his pistol.

The cop was strong and quick though. He and Rum Rum struggled for the weapon. Redrum kneed the cop in the nuts and he fell but took control of the gun, stripping it from the dope mans' grip. Rum kicked the cop in the face with his steel toed brown lug boots and then took off running toward Lucky. The other cop finally shot the attack dog three times, Tat, Tat, Tat, killing Cyclona instantly.

Redrum instinctively ducked as the shots rang out. Tat! Tat! Tat! Pop! Pop! Pop! He felt his legs burning but continued trying to run, but he couldn't and he ate dust. He'd been shot. Trooper blasted at the cop who had shot Redrum and he hit him. The cop got a taste of his own medicine. Retaliation is a must where they come from-Pig or no pig. The killa mentality of these gangsters was kill em all and let God sort em out.

Dreamer was already on the next-door neighbor's roof, popping shots at the cops who were raiding the front door. He was waving Trooper over. "Come on homeboy.Jump! Get a running start and jump, I did it."

Trooper knew it was his only means of escape so he emptied the gauge and threw it off the roof and then sprinted, jumping, flying from one roof to the other on the run.

Lucky watched Trooper and Dreamer jump from rooftop to roof top until they were out of sight. The cops meanwhile were focused on the yellow house. Lucky was frozen in disbelief. He didn't know how to act or what to do. A black van came speeding down the alley, side door open with a masked man hanging out of the side, rifle in hand. Lucky was thinking 'now I've seen it all, cops doing drivebys.'

The cop hollered at Lucky, who was still on the wall, "Freeze motherfucker! Colton Police Department! Get your hands up now!" he ordered. The van screeched to a halting stop. Three other cops jumped out, weapons drawn.

"Get off that wall!"

"Hands up where I can see them!"

"Freeze, don't move!"

Each cop was giving separate orders confusing Tito. He didn't know what the fuck to do. He was scared out of his wits. Mind and heart racing, stomach aching, dripping sweat, thinking *damn, I can't go to jail now. I need a fix! I'm sick! Man what do I do? The homies shootin up the cops went all bad. This is a life sentence.*

The cops' orders and the mini 14 pointing at his gut, that if the cop decided to shoot him would send Lucky flying fifteen feet in the air and straight to heaven, brought him back to reality.

"Get your ass down here now!" they screamed, "Keep your hands up!"

Two of the cops went to assist their partners at the house. The cop pointing the mini-14 took his eyes off Lucky to see what his partners were doing. Lucky was within arm's reach of the cop, but looked over his shoulder to see who or what was in the backyard of the wall he was standing on. He prayed there were no dogs in that yard. Then he remembered that he had a knife and an eight ball of meth in his possession.

He thought to himself, *I can't get struck out for no bullshit.* He pumped himself up in his mind, *It's now or never and I aint doin life in a cell, fuck it!* The cop jumped at him and swung his rifle at Lucky's legs. He could have grabbed the cop's gun if he wanted. He knew what he had to do and he did it without hesitation. He made his move.

Lucky prayed that he'd live up to his name and 'get lucky.'

ROOKIE IN THE GAME
PAST-APRIL 1ST, 1985

Five months passed and Denise was released from jail. She came home to the Rose Gardens where Tito had rented another apartment, but this one was hidden toward the back of the complex so he'd have a chance at a quick slick get away if cops came looking for him. The Lopez family had Erik cremated. His ashes were in a bronze urn in Denise's room on her nightstand. A St. Christopher charm hung from the lid top. She kept a few Catholic candles lit as well. She'd put up pictures of her, Erik and Tito on the mirror, but the pictures were of when Erik used to be a good and sober person. That's the Erik that Denise was remembering. Not the dick, demon-possessed asshole who had almost murdered Tito.

Denise would hug the urn sometimes and talk to it as if Erik's ashes could actually hear her. She had fallen into a deep depression while in jail, mourning Erik's death and the loss of Tito and Zoe. She was on heat meds and in a zombie state, walking around in a daze with no direction. She slept all day and night for days at a time. Denise wouldn't even eat or shower unless Tito helped and pushed her to do so. She was so lost in her depression. She wasn't aware of too much going on around her. That's why she didn't notice the North Side Colton tattoo Tito had running down his forearm. She didn't even notice he was dressing gang related in khaki suits and white T's nowadays. Nor did she notice her little boy staying out all night, sometimes not even coming home for two or three days at a time. He was out running amok, hustling and jacking for that loot. Banging to show his gang brothers loyalty.

Since Tito was so young and he still looked innocent when he wasn't

G'd up, he became the OG's decoy for jack moves. He'd dress normally and bounce a basketball in front of the target dope man's house. Tito would knock on the dope house door and when the dealer's guard went down after seeing a little kid, the OG's guns would come out! Stomping through, catching the connect slippin, they'd clean out the spot for everything. That's the game Lucky Tito was playing while his mom was asleep at home.

You would have thought that Denise would have gotten a clue that her son was hustling when she opened the refrigerator and it was full of food and drinks. She knew damn well it had never been full when Erik was alive. *She* wasn't bringing any money in or collecting welfare for Tito or Zoe, since he was on the run and Zoe was living in a juvenile facility for abandoned children.

In fact, Tito had a new color TV and stereo, cd's, a new couch and other little things in the apartment. Denise shrugged it off though and went into the restroom. She opened the cupboard looking for toilet paper, but what she found was a syringe and an empty heroin balloon. Denise broke the needle and flushed both items. *I could've sworn I threw all Erik's paraphernalia away. Where did this shit come from,* she thought. She was in such a daze that she didn't even realize that she wasn't in the same apartment anymore. Nor did it cross her mind that the paraphernalia belonged to her son. She searched in the cabinet looking for Tito's Vicodine, which had been prescribed to him after his father half beat him to death. Tito ended up suffering a broken jaw, a concussion, a broken nose, a sprained wrist and thirty stitches all over his face and head. He was in pretty bad shape-but the kid was tough. It wasn't his first beating, but it sure was the last he'd endure by that dick of a father of his.

Lucky Tito came home late after hustling all day and went directly to his mom's room to check up on her. She was curled up asleep. He sat at her bedside and affectionately brushed her dirty, tangled hair with his hand. The expression on his face showed sadness and worry. He hated seeing his mom like this. He didn't want to lose her to a broken heart. He softly shook her waking her.

"Mom, get up. Come on. I got Big Macs and fries with ranch dressing, your favorite. Wake up moms, you've gotta eat something."

Denise rolled over and mumbled in a delusional state of mind, "Erik, where you been babe?" she asked as she pushed her hair out of her eyes.

Lucky Tito's nose and forehead wrinkled in anger at the mention of his dead father. He hated him with a deep passion. Lucky Tito never wanted to be like his father, a scandalous, no-hustle having tecato. The difference between Tito and his father, now that he was a dope fiend, was that Lucky Tito wasn't scandalous. He had hustle and Erik had been the opposite. Not only did his father get him hooked on heroin, but also Denise and the doctors didn't know that Erik had injected the heroin into Tito. For some reason he didn't tell his mom.

Lucky Tito was forced to grow up overnight. He already considered himself a man at the young age of twelve. He was already waiting on the next meth fiend to give him a page so he could serve them a sack and make some money. He wanted to make that money so that he could provide for his family like a *real* man does. As young as he was, he was handling business. He was taking care of his moms instead of her taking care of him and on top of everything-he was doing it better than his father ever had. Lucky Tito stayed on Redrum's side, jacking dope connects who were enemies of his hood. Then they would split the dope and sell it in the Rose Gardens. Lucky Tito also hung out with OG's like Sharky, Loco, Shorty and Bacon who also were into slamming heroin.

The young gangsters his age weren't into heavy drugs yet. They never touched heroin. They were drinking, smoking weed and maybe snorting a little speed every now and then. But none of them were slamming dope yet. Even though Lucky Tito had barely started banging and hustling, he was already ahead of his generation in the gang and dope game. The veteranos were drawn towards Lucky Tito and had him under their wings. Lucky Tito looked at life in a whole new perspective now. It's as if he had been blinded or gullible before that night his father had slammed heroin into his virgin veins. That night he received his vision of what life was all about. Lucky Tito's philosophy was this, 'Y*ou gotta play the cards and hand you were dealt. There's gotta be a winner and a loser.'* He was willing to do whatever it took to win at this game, including cheating. The cop's laws were irrelevant. He was now living according to the law of the streets. Living according to the hood's G-code. No snitching! Never fake it, just take it! Never bow down or be weak! Always be strong minded! Do what you gotta do to live, eat, come up, and most importantly, survive! Take care of the family, moms and your gang brothers. If your homie's in trouble being jumped, outnumbered or not, weapons or not, you jump in and help him. When one jumps-you all jump. There's no such thing as a fair fight. Life aint fair and good guys always seem to end up with the short end of the stick.

In Lucky Tito's mind he figured, as long as he wasn't physically hurting anyone while he came up on the goods, money and dope, then there was no reason to feel guilty about living the life of a criminal. He still had a good heart, but he was damaged goods. His heart was broken because of what his father had done to him. Most of all, because of what his moms was going through now.

Mourning his father's death was too overwhelming for her to handle. She was physically weak and weak minded as well. Lucky Tito felt that he might have enough strength for the both of them. He was getting street smart. He was sly, slick, sharp and strong minded. He'd follow his mind now and not his broken heart. The thing was though, that his mind and body were addicted to heroin and it was possible that he could make a mistake that could cost him his freedom or life. He didn't trust and listen to his broken heart because if he did that then he would have committed suicide by now. Either that or become half-dead and depressed like his moms, laid out in bed just rotting away. Denise really needed to be saved and helped. But Lucky Tito had no idea how to snap her out of her depression.

Tito could smell his mom. She needed a shower. He was hand feeding her fries and soda saying, "Here moms, sip this soda. I'll put ketchup on your Big Mac."

Denise opened her eyes in a daze saying, "Mijo I was dreaming of your pops. I miss..."

She started sobbing uncontrollably, dropping her Pepsi on the floor. She curled up into the fetal position. Lucky Tito threw a towel on the floor, cleaned it up and then sat down next to his mom, comforting her, cradling and hugging her as tight as possible, not wanting to let her go. As if he did, she might slip farther away into a world of insanity. He whispered in her ear, "Don't trip moms, it's ok. I know it hurts your heart. Pops is ok though. He's doing better than we are though. Now he's in heaven with Jesus and the angels in paradise. All we can do is live one day at a time. Everything will be ok. You still have me moms. I'm still here. I'll take care of you."

Tito secretly resented his father though. He hoped Erik was in Hell, burning-being tortured by the devil himself. But he had to comfort his moms. Denise buried her face in Tito's chest, hugging him and sobbing, "I love you mijo, you're a good kid. You'll be a cop one day and get us out of here. I know you will," she said and she fell asleep.

Lucky Tito thought to himself, *I'll get us out of here, but it won't be by becoming a cop.* Denise was hiccupping in her sleep. Tito put a red blanket on her and fixed her pillow. Then he tucked her in nice and comfy, kissing her on the forehead and saying a quick prayer for her.

The radio was playing quietly, Art Laboe's oldies show was on and the song, "How Can You Mend a Broken Heart," by Al Green[ii] was playing.

Tito wished he knew how to mend a broken heart. All he knew was how to block the pain in his heart temporarily by slamming heroin. Tears shed his eyes as he stared down at his moms. He held his pain in and wiped his tears away. Usually he had his own way of dealing with his pain and emotional rollercoasters. He would get high to escape reality. But this time, he was fed up. He took down the pictures of his pops, grabbed the bronze urn full of ashes and headed to the restroom. As soon as he locked the restroom door, Lucky Tito seemed to fall into a world of insanity. He started talking to his father's ashes, spirit, or soul if he had one, as if he was there with him. Lucky Tito was flashing back to when he and his father were last in the restroom together in his old apartment. Lucky Tito tore up his pops' pictures then pulled out a cigar filled with Indo weed. He split it open with his knife and then opened his father's urn and sprinkled his pops' ashes into the blunt cigar, lacing it with a taste of death, and rolled it back up tight. He lifted it up and smoked away as he threw his father's torn pictures and the rest of his ashes into the toilet.

Lucky Tito blew out a giant cloud of smoke, coughing and saying to his father's spirit, "Pops, do you see what you're doing to my mom's? Huh? Maybe if she aint gotta see your stupid face in those pics every time she wakes up, maybe she'll forget about ya stupid ass. Ya never did nothing good for us anyways!"

Tito unzipped his Khakis and pissed on his father's pictures, right on his face and ashes. Exhaling another cloud of smoke, feeling the high, he said, "Rest in piss pops! You piece of shit! I don't know why moms misses ya scandalous ass any old ways. All you ever did was steal her money and food stamps and sell our stuff for dope. You beat her and you beat me. All you were was a fuckin coward! I know you're in hell with your soul burning. I hope the pain you're feeling is 666 times worse than both of ours! You deserve worse. I'll tell you what pops-I'm going to get you high for ol time's sake."

Lucky Tito laughed, hella loaded as he pulled out a fat chunk of black tar heroin that was going to take him to the next level. Tito peeled a few pieces off and threw them into the toilet for his pops saying, "There goes a few crumbs for your crumb snatchin ass pops. All you are is a nat on a dog's dick!" Then he flushed the torn pictures and the rest of the ashes down the toilet.

Lucky Tito had already slammed a shot an hour before he came home. That, plus the potent indo he had in him, had him in a delusional state of mind. He was strong, but he felt weak this night. He'd been holding everything that had happened to him in and it was all coming out now. Now that it was just him and his pops' spirit in the restroom-and the drugs that allowed him to see his pops' spirit. Lucky Tito was having a mental break down. He imagined his fiend of a father's spirit on his knees, digging in the toilet for the dissolving chunks of dope, which was torture to a fiend. Lucky Tito was laughing, yet tears were running down his cheeks. He was on a mixed emotional roller coaster.

He yelled out, "Burn in hell pops! Your bitchass been gone five months and I aint missed you at all. The devil paints a pretty picture of you to moms to keep her sad. I recognize Lucifer's only got moms remembering the good you, before you were a fiend. But I remember the bad you, the devil in you. The you who slammed heroin into me! I'm gonna paint a picture of the real you to her. I'm gonna tell her what you did to me. I'll help her remember the sick, evil you became. All the beatings we took just cuz you were sick or high!"

Lucky Tito repeated the weed smoking ritual. Inhale, exhale, until the blunt was almost gone. Then he said, "I have your ashes in my lungs pops. You're gonna become a part of me now. You're gonna become my slave. I'm gonna punish you and break your spirit pops."

Tito put the toilet seat down and sat on it. He pulled his blue bandana out and tied off his arm so he could fix a shot of dope. He already had a full syringe ready. Sticking it into the bulging vein in his right arm, he said, "Look pops; it's Lady Negra, your drug of choice. This must be torture for you huh pops. You wanna shot? I know you do. I bet you'd sell your soul for a fix huh? Just a little taste? Your soul's condemned. You can keep that garbage! How's it feel to want and not have? Haha! Yeah, that's the business from here on out. I'm the man of the pad, and a better one then you ever were, matter of fact you're *Erik* now. You're no longer pops."

Lucky Tito felt the heroin rush and he began to sweat. He almost felt like he wanted to throw up, overwhelmed with the euphoria of the high. He wet the bandana and wiped his forehead and face clean.

Lucky Tito mumbled, "Your ashes turned into smoke are glued to my lungs. You're inside me now, and I ain't letting you cross over." He took the last toke of the blunt until it felt like his lungs would explode. He held it in for as long as possible. Lucky imagined he was casting some sort of black magic spell with his words, binding his father's spirit. Intertwining his spirit with his father's…capturing him. He felt the spell's exchange take place within himself. He felt powerful. *HE* was the dominating one now. Lucky Tito opened his red bloodshot eyes, strolled over to the mirror and stared at himself. He smiled as his suspicions were confirmed. He'd seen his father's eyes within his own. His countenance kept changing back and forth, looking like his father, then himself. He finally exhaled the last hit of Indo and saw his father's face in the cloud of smoke. He wished his father's memory could disappear that easily. He grinned because before he swung at the cloud, his father's face was in agony, screaming. But Tito only heard the terrified screams in his own head.

He wiped his tears away, feeling warm and lovely inside. He said, "This feels good huh pops? It's your last high so enjoy it."

Lucky Tito wiped the blood drops from his arm and wiped away the sweating bullets. He sat on the bathtub and lit a cigarette saying, "Now every time I slam dope, you'll feel the needle poke, Pops but not the high or the rush. How do you feel about that? Yeah, I know that's fucked up huh? Ha-ha oh well, but you fucked up so Im'a torment you in as many ways as I can think of. Even if I gotta hurt myself to hurt you mothafucka. Fuck your ass!"

Tito lay in the bathtub, hallucinating.

"Guess what Erik, today's my twelfth birthday. Aren't you gonna sing to me? I know, I know you ain't been singing to me, but I control your spirit now, so sing you stupid fuckin bastard...on three ok. One...two...three...sing!" Tito started singing to himself and imagined his good Pops standing over him, holding a white cake with a number twelve candle lit up on it singing, *Happy birthday to you, Happy birthday to you, Happy birthday dear Tito, Happy birthday to you.*

Tito got lost in his high, nodding out, celebrating his twelfth birthday as the newest rookie in the game.

WELCOME TO THE MAJORS
PRESENT DAY, MAY 5TH, 2008-6:25 A.M.

Officers Yang and Lara were parked at the Arco Gas Station on Valley and La Cadena Drive. They'd just arrested a 211-robbery suspect. The Crip gang member was sitting in the back seat of the police cruiser, sweating and complaining about his handcuffs being too tight. It was one of these officers' easiest busts. They were dealing with one of the world's dumbest criminals. Half an hour prior, both officers had been eating breakfast at the Denny's Restaurant, which was 30 yards away from the Arco when the robbery in progress call came crackling through their shoulder radios. Officer Lara was getting a coffee refill when from his peripheral vision he spotted the 211 suspect sprinting behind the Denny's and running into the Naugal Restaurant restroom. It was as simple as running up and knocking on the door and saying, "Hurry up in there, I gotta take a shit!"

The robber, who was now dressed differently than when he had run into the restroom, opened the door. His eyes bulged out of his eye sockets when he walked into two glocs pointing at his face.

Officer Lara was sitting in the driver's side of his police cruiser, tapping at the computer keys. His partner Yang was cleaning and sealing up evidence bags on the front hood of the cruiser. He double-checked his initials and tagging of evidence, which were a nine-millimeter Ruger and a 16 round clip with three rounds missing. The casings were gathered and bagged at the scene. Those were warning shots by Rasheed Thomas to scare the store clerk into giving up the loot. There was a silencer on the tip that kept the gunshots muffled.

There were 630 dollars of legit stolen money and another 500 of counterfeit that Rasheed already had. It was a bad job of counterfeiting too. The money didn't even look real, but that was the only money that was logged into evidence. The 630 dollars stolen from the Arco went into officer Yang and Lara's pockets. The last item tagged was a black ski mask.

The clerk when questioned had stated, "The robber was black. I didn't see his face because he had on a black ski mask, but he talked black."

All the evidence went into the trunk, and then Officer Yang sat in the passenger seat next to his partner. He looked back at Rasheed Thomas and whistled saying, "You're going to be doing a lot of time brother man."

Officer Lara added, "The silencer alone is ten years. Plus the warning shots automatically add 20 years. Gun enhancements, counterfeit money, ten more years. Man Rasheed, You're pretty much fucked you moron! And we ain't even thrown the robbery into the equation yet."

Officer Yang laughed and said, "The gun laws are barring you dumb asses who stole pistols. You should've just murdered the clerk. You would've gotten less time and probably wouldn't be sweating bullets on your way to West Valley Jail."

Rasheed Thomas was agitated and nervous. His mind was racing, trying to figure a way out of this jam. He knew these two cops were corrupt and dirty. Everyone in Colton knew about Yang and Lara.

Rasheed blurted out, "Come on y'all. Do a brotha righteous. Give a nigga a chance. Everyone knows y'all be ridin dirty, shaken niggas down fo loot. Taxin till it hurts. Peep hustle. If y'all got jack moves, I know where a kilo be. Peep low key it's on the apartments on Rancho and Mill."

Officer Yang asked, "The Zoo or the Rose Gardens?"

Rasheed spit it out quickly, "The Zoo ma nigg. My nigga Young Devil scored that sheeit. Da niggas ballin-pushin major weight. But he aint kickin but crumbs and pebbles so fuck em. Y'all hit em and come up!"

Officer Lara asked, "What do you know about that 187 in the Rose Gardens last week?"

Rasheed looked like he was contemplating giving up the murderer. He weighed the consequences out in his mind. Giving up a dealer was one thing, but giving up a killer was playing Russian roulette and a for sure death sentence if word got out that he snitched. Rasheed felt he'd lost his life either way, so he spit out the info, gambling his life away. Rollin them dice he said, "It was that sick esay Crucifix who pulled that

187 on that Nazi white boy. Shot em all up on his swastika tattoo. Dats all I know. Crucifix erased that wood. Crucifix be crossin niggas up fo sho y'all." Officer Yang and Lara smiled and exchanged glances when they heard the info. Just then, an all-points bulletin came crackling over the radio.

"Officers down! Officers down! Location: Mt. Vernon and G Street. Be on the lookout for three suspects. Suspect one Hispanic male, approximate age 35, 6'1," wearing black pants and football jersey. Last seen running east on H street. Suspect may be armed and dangerous."

With that, the description of Tito was complete. Trooper and Dreamer's description came next, but they had already car jacked someone and were heading to Rialto to hide out.

Officer Yang shut his cruiser door and told his partner, "Let's take the long way to the station and go down 'H' street. We might get lucky knocking out two birds with one stone."

The black and whites sped off up the block, sirens off. A minute later, both cops spotted Lucky Tito Lopez who happened to fit the APB description of the suspect. Tito was looking paranoid. He was eyeing the block, standing in front of 'The Rock', a local church. A pastor opened the front door and he and Tito began talking. Tito was looking over his shoulder nervously, making hand gestures to the pastor as if explaining something to him. The pastor put his arm around Tito and escorted him into the church, shutting the door behind them.

The two corrupt cops' hearts simultaneously pumped hate and envy. Lara's blood began to boil hot as soon as he spotted Tito. Officer Yang picked up his radio to report the location of the suspect, but Lara pulled the radio away from his partner, short stopping the call.

Corrupt officer Lara looked dead serious and anxious as an idea popped into his head. He whispered, "I gotta better idea bro. Today is Tito's last day on these streets. Ol Lucky's luck is about to run out. He's about to catch strike three, which will assure he does life this time. No ifs, ands or buts about it. No slipping through the cracks this time. I put that on my life partner, he's through. Just follow my lead."

Officer Yang nodded in agreement and Lara pulled his cruiser off into the alley across the street from the church to await Tito's exit.

In the alley, the dirty pig's set-up plan began to unravel and come into effect. Officer Lara and Yang walked to the back of the cruiser and opened the trunk, and then Lara began unzipping evidence bags that belonged to Rasheed Thomas. Lara ran down the details of his plan to Yang, who grinned evilly and chuckled when he saw his partner screwing the silencer back onto Rasheed's pistol. Lara laughed as he popped in the clip and cocked one bullet into the chamber.

Officer Yang pulled Rasheed Thomas out of the cop car and pushed him against a grey brick wall near a green city dumpster. The coast was clear, only a few dogs were barking along the alley.

Yang told Rasheed, "Look Crip boy, today's your lucky day. We want Tito Lopez more than we want you. Plus you gave up two people so you get your second chance, but you gotta do as told or the deal's off and you do life in prison. We're going to let Tito ride your gun and robbery beefs, but you gotta be a witness saying you were in the vicinity and saw him hold up the Arco Gas Station. How do you feel about that?"

Rasheed felt hope once again and quickly answered, "Yeah cuz, fo sho. I'm wit it cuz whateva y'all want. Y'all da bosses."

Officer Lara came to stand at Yang's side. He had the nine Ruger concealed behind his back. Rasheed felt bad vibes. The cops were giving him good news with their mouths, but their eyes were telling a completely different story. He felt something was wrong.

Rasheed nervously blurted out, "Yeah dat sound cool cuz. Have esay ride da beef. I hate Mexicans anyway cuz, fo sho."

Trouble was brewing in his gut when Officer Lara pistol-whipped Rasheed. His ears were ringing as he spit out teeth and blood.

Lara yelled, "You don't like Mexicans huh? Well I'm a Mexican! Now you got a reason not to like Mexicans. Hate me now cuz," Lara taunted him. "Do I look like a fuckin Crip to you fuckin asshole? I'm not your fuckin cuz idiot! So quit calling me cuz!"

Rasheed curled up like a coward and groaned out in pain, "I ought to sue y'all corrupt poleezez fo brutality. Damn mane, why y'all trippin on lil shit." Rasheed was still cuffed and tried to stand.

Officer Yang kicked and clipped Rasheed's legs, dropping him. Then Yang pulled out his Billy club and beat Rasheed like he was Rodney King. Yang yelled, "You fucked up now threatening us!"

Lara had his arms folded keeping point and said, "Shut the fuck up, quit crying. You're a coward and a rat. Rule number one, don't trust a rat, matter fact, we're switching over to plan B. Tito's still gonna still take the rap, but for *your* murder."

Yang quit beating on Rasheed who groaned, "What murda, I aint kill nobody." He was bleeding badly and out of breath and stuttered, "What y'all want, I'll do it."

Lara said to Yang, "Wow Yang, I think you gave the Crip brain damage. He still don't get it."

Officer Lara walked over to Rasheed, pointing the 9 millimeter at his face and said, "When I said your murder rap, I meant your death. YOUR execution. Sorry for the confusion CUZ."

Lara mimicked Rasheed's slang as he pulled the trigger and sent him to Hell. Lara looked at his watch and told his partner, "Tito Lopez murdered Rasheed Thomas at 6:44 a.m. Happy Cinco De Mayo cuz boy."

The silencer had muffled the murder sounds to whispers, which lead the demons to pick up another soul.

The dogs at the end of the alley were barking up a ruckus. They probably smelled death in the air. Officer Yang uncuffed Rasheed Thomas and he and Lara picked the corpse up and threw it in the dumpster. They entered the cop cruiser and bumped knuckles laughing.

Lara said, "That's 25 to life for the gun, 25 to life for the robbery, strike three, and 25 to life for the murder. Tito's out."

Yang winked saying, "That should hold him huh partner?"

Officer Lara pulled the cruiser up about 20 yards in the alley so he could get a better view of the church and see when Tito left. He turned on the radio adjusting the volume to low, and settled in, listening to an oldie by Etta James.[iii] It reminded him of his first love, Tina Espinonza. The lyrics went,

'Something told me it was over, when I saw you and him walking by. Something deep down in my soul said cry, cry boy... I'd rather go blind than to see you walk away from me'.

This song reminded Officer Lara of the day he'd caught his girlfriend Tina with Tito Lopez, Lara's childhood best friend. He'd rather have gone blind than to see what he saw that day. The song hypnotized official Lara as he took a trip down memory lane.

The year was 1990. Alex Lara was in his junior year at Colton High School. He was enrolled in the Junior Explorers Police Program, learning all the ins and outs of pursuing a career as a police officer. He'd go on ride-alongs with Colton PD cops on the weekends. Alex was deeply in love with Tina Espinoza. She'd been his girlfriend for two and a half years and Alex planned to marry Tina after they graduated from high school. He had it all planned out, marry Tina, join the police academy and live happily ever after.

Alex had always had a crush on Tina, ever since elementary school. They'd grown up together in the Rose Gardens Apartments. She was with his best friend, Tito Lopez, during that time. They probably would have stayed together, but Tito was caught up when he was 13 years old and was sent away to Youth Authority. Tito was arrested for murdering his foster parents and kidnapping his sister Zoe. He beat the cases though, claiming that he'd escaped the murderers' grip. Since the other two kids weren't hurt, the story stuck. He was still sent to Youth Authority though, for guns and drug charges. One year into his term, Alex and Tina 'accidentally' became a *thing*. It just so happened that they both had love and respect for Tito, and it was them writing letters together to Tito that kind of drew them closer. The day Alex asked Tina to be his girlfriend, she'd accepted. Her one condition, however, was that they both write Tito a respectful letter to let him know that they'd gotten together, stressing that they didn't plan it, that they weren't trying to play Tito or make him look like a fool. Tina hit up a p.s., mostly expressing that she was not trying to hurt Tito and she still loved Tito and that she always would. Alex didn't see the p.s. though because she'd quickly sealed the letter and sent it off.

Tito got the letter, smirked, tore it up and flushed it in his cell toilet. He shut down and never wrote back. Tina knew the letter hurt Tito, so she secretly began writing Tito again and sending him pictures of her. She sent poems and money that she got from Alex. Alex took good care of Tina, giving her money, jewels, clothes and whatever else her little heart desired. He tried buying Tina's love because he knew Tina still loved Tito. They were each other's first loves and Alex felt bad, but took advantage of the opportunity because he loved Tina too. No matter how hard he tried, she never looked at Alex like she did Tito. Either way she still had Alex's heart. Tina wrote to Tito three times a week, and every week she received three *return to sender* letters back. She just put them away and vowed to make Tito read them all when he paroled. Tito secretly read them though and sealed them back up to make it look as if they had never been opened.

Colton High School was having a dance and Alex had bought Tina a pretty dress to wear-one that would have all the dudes' tongues hanging out of their mouths, drooling. Alex was proud of Tina's fineness. He loved holding her hand at school and showing her off.

That day, he walked into Tina's apartment unannounced trying to surprise her, but *he* was the one who got surprised. Tears filled his eyes and his right hand instinctively covered his broken heart at what he saw.

Tito had paroled early and when Alex walked in, Tina and Tito were in bed making love and she was moaning, "I love you Tito. I wanna marry you babe, I love you with all my heart!"

Tito smiled when he saw Alex walk in the room. He hadn't even bothered to push Tina off him. She rode him slow, yet rough. Tito grabbed her hips and made her grind harder, evilly grinning as Tina moaned adding insult to Alex's injury. Then Tito spoke out, saying, "Payback's a bitch." Then he'd told Alex, "This shit's killing you huh Alex? Ha-ha!"

Tina had turned around. She had looked embarrassed when she'd seen Alex standing in a dazed shock, tears running down his cheeks.

Tito had held Tina in place saying, "What goes around comes around Alex. She was mine before she was yours playboy. Gracias for keeping the snatchola warm dawg, but daddy's home so move around with the sad face and tears."

Alex felt humiliated and a deep hatred blossomed in his heart for Tito. It's as if he now hated Tito as much as he loved Tina. He looked at Tina's naked body and remembered the last time he had made love to her, and knew he'd never get that chance again.

He was speechless until he'd blurted out, "Is it over Tina? After all I've done for you. You're gonna play me like this and treat me like shit?"

Tina blushed with embarrassment. She put her head in the pillow, hiding like an ostrich does, hoping and pretending her problem wouldn't see her and would go away. She felt ashamed though.

Tito had put his hand on Tina's chin and lifted it up saying, "Look the man in the eyes and answer him."

Tina's eyes teared up when she turned and saw the pain in Alex's eyes. She had love for Alex, but she wasn't in love with him anymore.

She finally answered, "I'm sorry Alex I love Tito. You know that I always have, it aint no secret. He's home now. You know what's up. I'm sorry I hurt you."

Alex had yelled at Tina and Tito, "Fuck you both!"

Tito laughed and said, "I'll fuck you later Alex, I'm fucking Tina right now, you punk ass bitch! Get the fuck outta here you crybaby."

Then Tito turned Tina over and started sexing her up. Maybe even grudge fucking her for fucking with Alex while he was away. You know what they say, while the dogs away, the cats come out to play.

Alex had walked away, heart shattered to pieces, feeling like a lame idiot. That day Alex Lara promised himself that he'd become a cop and lock Tito Lopez up in prison for life. His goal in life was to bury Tito alive in a cell, knowing he'd never see the streets or be with Tina again. But that kind of slow death was too easy for Tito. Alex wanted Tito to suffer in pain for the rest of his life on death row.

Officer Yang tapped Officer Alex Lara's shoulder, "Hey bro, snap out of it. Earth to Alex! Come in Alex."

Alex Lara returned from memory lane and turned off the radio disgustedly saying, "What's going on bro? Where's Tito?"

Officer Yang answered, "No sign of him yet. Do you want to go in and get him?"

"Nah man, we'll wait. Patience is a virtue. The best things come to those who wait."

Right then the church's front door opened and both officers cocked back their weapons. The two pigs were the definition of corrupt cops. L.A. Rampart-Division didn't have nothing on these two.

Tito's heart was still pounding. The adrenaline had him dry heaving and looking for a trash can to throw up in.

Pastor Rick handed him one and told him, "Sit down Tito. Relax, calm down son. Who are you running from? You look as pale as if you've seen the devil himself."

Tito was sweating bullets looking around all paranoid. He looked up to see an 80-year-old man with a full head of white hair. He wore a Crimson colored sweat suit and a gold cross chain hanging down. He offered Tito a cup of water and Tito downed it thirstily.

"I'm running from the cops, he said. I need to lay low for a minute. Thanks for the agua."

Pastor Rick sat in the pew at Tito's side. He looked him in the eyes and said, "Tito, aren't you tired of always running from the cops and your enemies? Son, you're your own worst enemy and you'll never outrun yourself. Your flesh is trying to outrun your spirit and that isn't possible. You're trying to run from God Tito, and He has big plans for you. Your mama's been saved now for 20 years. She stopped running but you're long overdue."

Tito stood up stretching, feeling a bit guilty saying, "I had plans to go to a sober living home or a Victory Outreach Rehab as soon as I paroled, but I got caught up again. Next thing you know, I was slamming Black again strung out. I'm sick and tired of being sick and tired. I can't even think straight. I'm in a church and I'm thinking of slamming some crystal to get right! But the cops raided my connect. I already got two strikes, so if I get hemmed up, that's strike three. The pigs shot Big Rum Rum. Trooper and Dreamer busted on the pigs. Everything happened so fast. I was just there for a balloon of dope."

Tito's knees gave out on him and he fell face first onto the floor, hands covering his eyes. He began sobbing deeply. Tears flooded his eyes with frustration.

Pastor Rick kneeled down at Tito's side and put his arm under Tito.

He placed his hand on his heart and began praying, "Father God, help your child Tito. He needs you to heal his body of his addictions. Take his sickness away Lord! Take those evil urges away in Jesus Christ's name. Let Tito desire your grace and love. Warm his heart full of your joy and love, give him your gift of salvation. Save him from this hell on earth lifestyle he's living. Open his heart and eyes Jesus. Let him see that the devils pulling the puppet strings that control his evil deeds, Lord cut those puppet strings now! Set Tito free in your precious name, Jesus I bind all devils and demons out of Tito's life! In Jesus' name, I command you all back to the pits of hell! Flee! Amen."

Tito felt chills going through his body. He almost felt high. A high he had never felt before. He felt a weight, a burden, rise off his shoulders. His bones no longer ached. He felt at ease, even a bit joyful, as if God himself had kissed his forehead and showed him love and forgiveness.

Tito prayed, "Lord God thank you if this is you. I'm sorry. I want to get right and live how you want me to live. Come into my heart Jesus! Please save me!" Tito cried his heart out for five more minutes. He was convinced that he finally felt God's precious holy presence. He felt better than any high he'd ever experienced.

Tito stood and took off his wife beater, exposing a strung out tattooed body.

Pastor Rick hugged Tito saying, "You're saved now brother. That's the good news. You're a warrior for God now. The bad news is the Devil is pissed at you and you're now his enemy so he's going to come back and attack you quickly. He'll tempt you. He'll bring back urges for dope and try to make you fall. It's an ongoing battle but you're aware of the Devil now. So call on God and fight the urges! Pray, read the bible. Call a Christian brother when you feel weak, to help you."

Tito cut Pastor Rick off, "Look, I need to go to a Christian rehab home right now so I can kick this dope. I can't do it myself out here. I feel better right now, but I'll be fiending for a fix tonight. I need to go far away where I don't know of any dope spots."

Pastor Rick reached in his pocket, pulled out a cell phone and dialed a phone number. He talked for a minute then hung up. Pastor Rick said, "Okay Tito, I have a friend, Pastor Sal, who has a Christian home in Indio with Victory Outreach. He's agreed to take you in. It's in the middle of the desert, so if you try to escape there's no fences, but it's a 15-20 mile walk to the first city. I know you aren't trying to go through all that." He patted Tito's shoulder. "We'll get you the help. Let me lock up here and I'll drive you to Indio. Do me a favor and go to the alley and throw that trash can full of throw up away."

Tito picked up the trashcan, smelling his own vomit. He asked, "So I'm really saved from Hell now pastor Rick?"

Pastor Rick nodded yes.

Tito said, "You're a good man. You helped save my mom, and now me. My word I'm gonna really try to live right and live for God, since Jesus died for me, it's the least I could do right?"

Pastor winked at Tito and pointed to the door, "Hurry Tito."

Tito stepped outside feeling brand new, taking a deep breath of fresh air. He actually noticed the beautiful blue sky and admired the clouds and hummed along with the birds singing in the trees. He heard a lawnmower at work and smelled the freshly cut grass. He was amazed at this new feeling and he was thinking things were going to be different now. Finally, he was going to be free!

Then he strolled into the alley and the first thing that he noticed was blood and flesh on the gravel next to the dumpster. Tito tried to open the dumpster but it wouldn't open, so he looked over the side of the huge can and there he saw a pair of handcuffs locking the dumpster lid in place.

Just then, he heard a 5.0 cop car engine speeding up behind him. He turned quickly dropping the trashcan just as Alex Lara and Yang lunged at him. When he saw the two pistols pointing dead on him he threw his arms up!

LINE DRIVE
PAST-FEBRUARY 7TH, 1990

Tito was in his restroom, wiping his sweat away. He'd just done a thick shot of heroin and made it to his bed to lie down and enjoy his nod. While he lay there, his mind drifted off as he went on a trip down memory lane. This vision scared him. He went back to the day four years earlier when he was arrested and his whole Youth Authority term kicked in. Tito remembered Redrum and Trooper telling him, "This is gonna be an easy hit. This aint nada dog,"

Trooper, who was around Tito's age, said, "We're young Tito. We're no real threat in the enemies' eyes. Believe that we're wolves in sheep's clothing though dawg. We got this well played with the soccer ball in front of the dope spot. Same game, like we're lil kids."

Redrum said, "But your baby, Jacka-G's creepin on a come up. Plus we've got you covered 100%, all the way around."

It didn't take much to talk Tito into rolling on the home invasion. He was hungry for moola green. He just needed the blue prints. The lil homie was with the business and on board for the hit. But this was real life, on the real side; things don't always go according to plan. This is how things went sideways and Lucky Tito got hemmed up and earned himself a trip to Youth Authority. Tito was remembering being in enemy territory West Side, San Bernardino. He'd been kicking the ball down 7th St. to Trooper who was running up ahead, playing his part. Both looked like innocent kids at play, only these two young jackers had .25 semi-automatics in their pockets, ready to pop the pistol, never thinking the hood would take them under.

The ruthless crew of Colton G's, North and East united, were packed into two vans with tinted windows and parked close by. Northsiders:

Scarface, Flaco, Shorty and Happy were in one van. In the other were the Eastsiders: Bandit, Romer, Strangler and Listo. All of them were fully strapped with Uzis, M-1 Carbines, AK 47's and hand guns cocked and ready. Ski masks and bandanas covered their faces to hide their identities. Their trigger fingers were ready, itching to pull triggers. The jackers were set on robbing all money, jewels and drugs, guns and anything worth any kind of loot. Little did the G's know, but the dope house that they were about to hit was under surveillance by S.M.A.S.H. (Street Marshals Against Street Hoodlums), Gang Suppression Task Force. The cops were a little deeper than the gangsters were. The cops were in an abandoned house across the street and posted up in unmarked cars, surrounding the block. San Bernardino PD had gotten a tip that a suspect they had been hunting for had been seen at the dope house. The suspect was wanted for homicide. These cops meant serious business.

The San Bernardino drug dealers had been hearing rumors from their customers about a string of robberies happening from Verdugo Flats to the Westside. They told them that what looked like two little kids playing ball were really in cahoots with the jackers, so they also had an eye out for them. The dealers were posted up and heated as well. They were on alert for another jacker crew too called the 2-Fivers, or Cinqueros, who were Sureno dropouts and had been green-lighted. Since the Mexican Mafia had put contracts out on them, they had nothing to lose. They became fools with no rules. The 2-Fivers focused on jacking any and all dope dealers who sold drugs for the Mexican Mafia. Drowsy from West L.A. Criminals and Chunky from Verdugo were running this crew of jackers. They even took Mafioso's hostage for ransom, having all their dealers drop off money and dope to other 2-Fivers in the Cinquero circle.

All this was in play that day so all dope dealers were on point. A Westsider, Joker, was on the porch smoking a cigarette when he saw Lucky Tito and Trooper kicking the ball up the street. He recognized game and opened the front door of the house and said something to the people inside. Then he reached in his pocket and pulled out his 9-millimeter pistol. Taking the safety off, he casually held it behind his leg. Trooper kicked the ball into the dope man's yard and sprinted towards it. Joker threw his smoke aside and pointed his pistol at Trooper and Lucky Tito.

Joker yelled, "Here, let me help you lil Puto!" Pop! Pop! Pop! He fired his gun at them both. They ran, ducking behind a car.

Lucky Tito hollered, "Fuck dog I'm hit!" He was shot in his right hand.

Trooper pulled his and Lucky Tito's pistol out and told Tito, "Shoot with your left hand and keep moving!"

Both baby gangsters began popping hot rocks at Joker who was standing right in the open yard as if he was bullet proof. Joker took three shots in the neck and chest that dropped him. He began to crawl away to safety as the situation quickly got worse. Gunfire came from inside the house. Automatic gunfire RARARARARARA - not no Pop-Pop-Pop shit. These dealers sent killer bees in Tito and Trooper's direction. The two vans of Colton G's drove up hella quickly, doors already open, poppin shots at the dope house, covering their little rider homie's backs. Redrum jumped out and pushed Trooper towards the open door of the van then He sprinted to safety. Lucky Tito was panicking because of all the blood leaking from his paralyzed hand. He was out of bullets. He moved away from the van, because the bullets were ricocheting off the cars he was hiding under. He was hit two more times in his leg and ankle. Adrenaline pushed him to keep moving, even though he was only hopping.

One van tried to swoop up to Lucky Tito, who wasn't feeling too lucky right about then. The fully autos were spitting back to back and he felt like he was in a war zone. The kid was against all odds. All he could think of was baby Zoe and his moms. They needed him. Redrum jumped up and let off a 50 round clip at the house. The enemies came back with a deadly 100 shots. The 100 round drum tore through the vans tires. Flaco, Scarface, Shorty, Happy and Trooper quickly jumped out the van, letting off every bullet they had. It was the Devil banging on the door, trying to get out of hell. Happy threw two grenades at the dope house, which bought them a few seconds to get to the Eastsiders' van who were letting pistols shout. There were screams and shouts coming from the house as explosions tore that ass up.

Just when they had the frontline sewed up and Tito felt hope and saw a way out, things got worse and then went all to hell. This all went down in a matter of 60 seconds or so. All of a sudden from behind him and Redrum, the Gang Task Force came running out of a house. Undercover cop cars swarmed the scene, blue and red lights on and sirens screaming. Tito knew it was every man for himself now.

Redrum at his side said, "Let's bounce lil homie. We gotta get ghost now!"

Lucky Tito groaned, "I can't Rum, I'm shot. Just bone out dawg. Go!"

Cops were moving in, hollering, "Freeze motherfucker, freeze!"

Redrum pulled his chain and crucifix of Jesus off and put it in Lucky Tito's hand. "Pray my boy, pray. I'm gone!" He told Tito.

Redrum was looking at the van with his riders waiting. He waved for them to leave and decided to flirt with death, running into his enemies' yard and began jumping fences out of bounds, even though he was three miles away from home. Lucky Tito threw his pistol under the car and acted as if he was just an innocent kid caught up in the crossfire.

Later that night he was cuffed to the bed at the Gilbert Street Hospital when we woke up. He lost consciousness soon after, and when he woke up again he was in Juvenile Hall. He found out he was set to fight a few serious cases. They'd charged him with the double homicide of his foster parents, Bill and Hope. They said he'd kidnapped his sister Zoe too. She was found in a gang sweep at the Rose Gardens and was placed in a Juvenile Facility Home. Lucky Tito was also fighting gun and drug charges, which were found within reach at the home invasion gone bad. The only two things that saved Tito were that number one, the cops saw Joker shoot at Tito first, and all then then all hell went bad. No cop could positively ID Tito as a shooter. The second thing that saved Tito on the double homicide charges was Bill and Hope's kids testified that they didn't see Tito or Zoe, but saw a few big Mexicans hurting their parents.

The kidnapping of his sister is what really sent him away to Youth Authority. Tito didn't care about the time. He was worried about his mom and baby sister. He got lucky in trial by not getting life. All the stuff he was going through woke up his mother Denise as well. Some people from Victory Outreach visited the juveniles in Juvie Hall and Tito had a talk with one woman and told her about his mother. That woman, Sister Kathy, began visiting Denise and helped her shake her depression. She showed her that she had to give her life to God and that Jesus would give her the strength to be there for her kids Tito and Zoe, who were both locked up. Sister Kathy was the cousin of Pastor Rick at The Rock church in Colton. He helped Denise as well. When Denise came out of her depressed stupor and reality kicked in, she realized she no longer had Tito or Zoe. The only one she had was Jesus Christ. Everything happens for a reason though. This was a good thing. Denise stopped using dope and got rooted in the word of the Bible, trying to live according to the Bible.

She was doing God's will for her life. She began living a Christian woman's life. All she could do was write to Tito in jail and accept his collect calls. She couldn't visit because she had a jail record now and that was against prison policy. She desperately wanted to hug Tito and tell him she was sorry for being weak and not being there for him. Denise used to send Tito Victory Outreach pamphlets. They'd have drawings on the front to get a person's attention. On the back page there would be a message about the Lord Jesus. She would tell Tito about the Bible and what it meant. Tito read everything, but didn't see how God fit into his life, even though he wore that chain and cross that Redrum had given him the day he was arrested.

There was another thing he didn't understand. How his big homie, Redrum, could be was so wild, a rider and killer, and all in the middle of a shootout give Tito a cross and tell him to pray. One time he collect called Redrum and asked him about that.

All Redrum did was laugh and say, "I'm God's son. I slay devils my lil brother. I'm my brother's keeper. No matter what I do, God's with me. The devil's my enemy lil G."

Lucky Tito still didn't understand Redrum's thinking, because Christians weren't supposed to live how Redrum lived. Maybe he was a radical Christian or something. He swore he saw demons everywhere, but the homies chalked it up as him being loaded on PCP, or maybe not.

Lucky Tito was still loaded and reached for his chain and cross and kissed it. He began itching all over. The heroin was doing what it do. He stood up in bed and reached over to a bag of mini Snicker's he had on the dresser. He took one down and lit up a Camel.

Tito was sitting up against the backboard of his bed and closed his eyes, remembering his Youth Authority teacher, Ms. Martinez. He mumbled to himself, *Rest in peace Martinez. I had love for you cuz you had love for me. I tried to keep my word and stay sober. You're gone now, so it shouldn't matter no more.* Lucky Tito remembered when he'd been in YA at a mandatory Narcotics Anonymous meeting. Ms. Martinez was running the meeting. She looked at the group and said, "What's said here stays here. I'd better not hear people's conversations or stories shared in this class being retold on the yard. That's your ass if I find out. Everyone show the speaker courtesy and respect and don't talk while they talk."

Lucky Tito had been to over a dozen meetings and never spoke or shared anything personal about himself or his addictions. All the class ever heard was his introductions.

"I'm Lucky Tito and I'm an addict."

Ms. Martinez said, "Today's topic is, *The First Time I Got High.* Say that sentence and then tell your story." Everybody started laughing, telling short stories, clowning. Lucky Tito sat quietly looking serious. Ms. Martinez noticed how uncomfortable Tito was and ordered the class, "Quiet down, quiet down. Everyone get serious now." All the young inmates mellowed out. Ms. Martinez said, "Tito Lopez, we'll start with you today."

Tito waved her off saying, "I pass."

Ms. Martinez shook her head, "Nope, you can't pass. If you refuse, I'll fail you, and you need this class to be released."

Tito turned red hot and pulled his hat down low over his eyes saying, "Whatever-fail me. I don't care." In reality, Tito really didn't care about going home. He was heartbroken. He'd lost his true love Tina, who'd betrayed him. The streets were all bad memories to Tito. He had no sister, no dad, and his mom was on some Jesus trip. In prison, he was guaranteed three meals a day and a bed. He didn't have to do nothing outrageous to get them. He had it coming mandatory.

Ms. Martinez said, "Just say something. You haven't spoken for over 12 meetings. You have to participate. This isn't a free ride."

Tito looked at her sideways as if she was irritating him. She saw she almost had him, so she said, "Just tell us the first time you got high and what your experience was like and you'll pass this class. You won't have to speak ever again, and there are four classes left."

Lucky Tito scratched at the track marks on his inner arm and paused for ten seconds, then said, "It was hell. The first time I got high was hell. My 'so-called' father was a heroin addict who beat my ass when I was 12, forced me to slam a shot, and then *he* slammed a shot when I was half-dead. Then he died of an overdose."

The classroom of inmates was dead quiet, just staring at Lucky Tito. Ms. Martinez's mouth was open and a tear ran down her eye as Tito spoke. She was used to these kids telling stories about smoking weed, maybe speed, but not heroin. There was an awkward silence in the classroom as Tito cleared the lump in his throat and took a deep breath to continue his story.

Only one of his enemies, Chico from Westside 7th Street disrespected him in mid-sentence saying, "That's how a prostitute gets hooked on dope, you hoe. Are you sucking dick for a fix now you leva? Haha."

Half the class laughed. The other half tensed up, knowing it was on! Chico had spit fighting words and Lucky Tito was no leva or a punk. Lucky Tito stood up and grabbed his chair charging at Chico, throwing it in his face full force, hollering, "Your mother's a leva and a puta you punk bitch!"

Tito pushed the chair out of the way then beat and stomped Chico's head into the ground. Chico was screaming for his homeboys to help him, but Tito's homeboys blocked them off saying, "It's one on one. Stay out of it unless you want a riot."

The enemy was outnumbered so they stayed out of the fight. Tito slugged away on Chico as if Chico was Erik. He spat on Chico saying, "Fuck you bitch. Fuck Verdookie and, fuck Sesame Street bitch!"

Ms. Martinez hit the alarm and staff swarmed in. The staff sprayed Tito with pepper spray and beat him with batons until he got on the floor and surrendered. Even then as he was escorted away, cuffed up feeling on fire he hollered, "Chico you're a leva! Now what poo butt?"

He laughed something wicked as they choked him all the way to the hole, where he'd stay for the next 45 days. After Lucky Tito was in the hole for about 30 days and had calmed down, Ms. Martinez got permission to pull Tito out and give him some counseling. She tried to get him to finish his story when it was just him and her, but he refused many times. She took an interest in Tito and seemed to be going the extra mile for the kid. She saw potential in him. She found out little by little that Tito had a good heart, but was just a victim of his environment and pretty much wasn't like the other juveniles in Youth Authority.

She gave him a little guidance to the right path. She molded and shaped Tito to become productive in society instead of becoming a menace to society. A year down the way, Tito finally opened up and told Ms. Martinez the rest of his story. How his dad forced dope into him, about how he lost his dreams of becoming a cop. How Tina broke his heart. How he found Zoe, his baby sister, crawling on her mother's overdosed dead body. He told Ms. Martinez that he felt like he seemed to be doing wrong or bad things for the right reasons and it was all for the love of his family and so that he'd survive on the streets. Tito wiped away his tears in their private sessions and felt better, finally letting it all out. Ms. Martinez spoke up for Tito Lopez at his board hearing and he was granted parole.

She saw Tito off on his release date, gave him a hug and told him, "Don't look back at this place or you'll be back."

Tito laughed and said, "Yeah, that's what they say, like Sodom and Gonora huh? I'll turn to stone or something right? Haha," he joked.

She said, "God bless you Tito, go to church and help the youngsters onto the right path. You don't have any excuse to go wrong or come back. Walk with the angels' mijo."

With that, Tito kissed her on her hand and said, "You were my angel." He smiled as did she, and he walked away clean, sober and feeling stronger and filled with hope.

Today was six months after Tito had paroled. He read in the newspaper that Ms. Martinez was found raped and murdered, dead in a dumpster on YTS Institution grounds. Her teacher's assistant was the prime suspect under arrest. This news broke Tito's heart. He loved and respected Ms. Martinez like an aunt. He couldn't get any retaliation unless he went to the County Jail, and that was a big maze and crazy mission.

He found himself at the heroin connection's buying a needle and a sack of dope after he read the news article. Now here he was, in bed, eyes leaking for his teacher, for his friend and NA sponsor. He was rubbing his cross, praying,

God I pray Ms. Martinez is with you if you even exist. Just make sure she ain't in pain no more. Let her be in heaven. She's one of your angels. She helped me. Help her God. Thank you.

He kissed his crucifix and pointed up to the sky saying, "I got love for you Ms. Martinez. Rest in peace."

Tito took a hit of his cigarette, opened his eyes and pulled a pistol out from under his mattress thinking out loud, *here we go again.*

R.B.I (RUNNING BACK INTO INSANITY)
PRESENT DAY, MAY 5TH, 2008-8:00A.M.

Lucky Tito's luck ran out. He was cuffed up by his old adversary, Alex Lara, who had the law as well as the firepower on his side. Officer Yang had his gun pointed at the back of Tito Lopez's head while his partner Lara searched Tito for weapons and paraphernalia. Lara was being rough with Tito too, kicking his legs apart, elbowing him in his back, slapping Tito from behind and giving him kidney shots, which took Tito's wind. To top it off Tito's kidneys were already shot because he had hepatitis. He felt helpless but refused to show weakness.

In fact, he provoked his ex-best friend when he searched Tito's front waistband. Tito said, "Go ahead and search my dick you faggot ass pig. I'm concealing two fat nuts for you there," he laughed.

Those were the wrong words. Officer Lara slugged Tito in the nut sack as hard as he could, buckling Tito to the ground.

Lara said, "Yeah you won't be fucking Tina with that little thing any time soon."

Tito was in a world of pain as Lara kicked the man while he was down and fully contained. Lara kicked Tito in the jaw and Tito really felt the pain.

Tito hollered, "Fuck you Alex! You aint about shit bitch. You hide behind that badge but you can't hide from the fact that you're scared of me. Give me a fair fight, pussy ass pig!"

Officer Lara backed up hollering, "I'm not scared of your skinny, dope fiend ass, you're a worthless piece of shit! I can't believe we were ever best friends as kids." Lara kicked Tito in the head.

Tito spit out blood and saw stars, shouting, "Fuck you pig, fuck you!"

Lara laughed, "Yeah, Yeah fuck me huh? Who has the last laugh now loser. Do you want to know something, Mr. 'Lucky'?" Lara motioned, making air quotation marks around the word '*lucky*'.

Lucky Tito rolled over still cuffed saying, "Nah I aint tryna hear nada you gotta say, cuz you don't even count in my world. Fuck what you feel and fuck what you're going through. Matter fact-fuck your life bitch. You'll get yours one day. Believe that fool! I put that on Colton! You'll bleed like I'm bleeding."

Officer Lara looked at his partner as he took off his belt buckle that held his weapon, cuffs, pepper spray and nightstick. He handed it to Officer Yang who put his own weapon in his holster and put Lara's equipment on the front hood of the cruiser.

Yang asked Lara, "Are you going to bite at this piece of shit's challenge? We got other plans. We don't have time for child's play. He's set up, let's do this."

Lara cracked his knuckles and told Yang, "We've got Lucky regardless. I want to call this idiot's bluff and see if he can walk how he talks, because I can. I'm going to beat his little fuckin ass. Uncuff him."

Yang shook his head in disagreement and strolled up to Tito kicking him in his ribs as hard as he could with his steel toe police boots hollering, "Turn on your stomach punk!"

Lucky Tito lost his wind and felt as if his ribs had just broken. The dogs up the alley were barking wildly now.

"You want a fair fight you got it. Then you're going to prison for life, so make sure you work out all your hate issues for me now punk ass bitch," Lara yelled.

Tito thought, *Fair fight Yeah right. Uncuff me after you break my ribs and jaw. Nothing fair about this, but I'm gonna get my bang on. Once in a lifetime chance.*

Tito was feeling even sicker now too from going through drug withdrawals, but he found it deep within to get to his feet, dust himself off and get ridin.

Just as the Pastor had just told him,

The Devil will come quick. If you fall, get up, dust yourself off and keep walking, knowing God's walking with you through anything and everything you're going through.

Remembering this gave Tito a new confidence and he knuckled up as if he was about to rumble a few rounds with the Devil himself. Lucky Tito heard sirens in the distance getting closer.

Officer Yang walked to the dumpster uncuffing the locks and opened it up saying, "Hey Tito here goes your life sentence. Premeditated murder, Twenty-five to life. You shouldn't have killed this Crip boy."

Tito eyed Lara, who had a wicked grin, and then Tito glanced in the dumpster seeing a dead black man. Lucky Tito finally realized what was going on. The ultimate set up. Lara pulled out Rasheed's gun with a silencer on it, pointing it at Tito who put his hands up hoping those sirens in the distance showed up quickly. He had a bad feeling.

Lara told Tito, "There's two bullets left in this gun. You can kill yourself here instead of going to prison."

Then Lara reached out to give it to Tito. Yang was standing behind Tito who looked back suspiciously. Tito knew there was a catch to this. Lara wouldn't hand Tito a loaded gun. But maybe he hated Tito that much that he'd allow him to kill himself. Who knew?

Lara said, "Either you kill yourself or I kill you." He cocked a bullet into the chamber.

Tito focused on Lara's black shooting gloves and his finger itching to pull the trigger.

Lucky Tito stood frozen thinking; *if I die, I go to heaven anyway.* He wasn't sure though that if he committed suicide it was a sin and if so then that would land him in Hell. He had a plan. Lucky Tito grabbed the gun from Lara.

"I'll kill myself, fuck it," Tito thought.

Yang already had his pistol pointed at Tito's back from a distance. Tito looked down the barrel of the pistol and said, "We both die Alex." Tito shot at Alex and turned the gun on himself, but nothing shot off. He was confused. Alex Lara stood there laughing, clapping his hands.

Officer Yang pistol-whipped Tito from behind, dropping him. Yang kicked the gun back to his partner Lara, who said, "That's gangster Lucky. You tried going out with a bang. I can respect that. But there were no bullets in the murder weapon and now YOUR fingerprints are all over the gun dumb ass. Now get up. We're going to go one round and then you're off to prison. Your street life is over and remember that, I, Alex Lara, made that happen." Lara put the pistol in his back pocket.

Yang kicked Tito, "Get up, we beat you! Now go take your medicine!"

Tito was having flashes of his wife, Tina, his son Lil Frankie and his mom Denise; it was all flashing before his eyes. He knew he was through, but he had to at least fight this devil Alex. Tito was in it too deep to quit now. He figured death was the only way out. The pigs or his.

Yang was flipping off Tito and laughing hella arrogantly. These were police officers acting this way. More like legalized gangsters. A city worker driving a street sweeper drove by slowly cleaning the street. He stopped briefly at the end of the alley and took off his orange vest while eyeing the officers and Tito. Then he drove on his way, continuing sweeping the street. This was a dead end alley, so it was a makeshift boxing ring type. Tito was on his feet walking toward Alex Lara.

Lara told his partner, "Only shoot him if he runs. No matter who's winning or losing, stay out of it Yang."

Both Tito and Alex collided, both making contact with their flying fists. Alex dropped to his knee first. Lucky Tito hit him with a few uppercuts, surprising Alex Lara. Since Alex had been trained in the Academy and knew Judo, he figured beating up Tito would be easy. Right about now he was discombobulated and figuring just the opposite. Tito rang his bell. Lucky Tito stomped on Alex who quickly rolled away out of it.

Lucky backed up bouncing on his tiptoes laughing, he said, "I've got the last laugh now puto! Get up, get up!" Tito and Alex circled each other.

Alex threw a punch, luring Tito's hands in to block it. He used that as a set up to open his temple and then Alex Lara made a six foot kick at Tito's head, spinning him. He then rushed Tito cracking him with a fast six to ten in the back of the head. Tito threw a back donkey kick right into Lara's stomach and followed up with a roundhouse when Lara buckled over.

Lara said, "You got Lucky, come on."

Lucky swung, answering, "That's why they call me Lucky."

Tito and Alex rushed each other again, both hitting the other. Connecting, shaking it off, they kept ridin, smashing each other up something vicious and looking like Mixed Martial Arts fighters. You could see their deep hatred for each other in their eyes.

Yang was sitting up on the hood of the cruiser, chewing on a toothpick, enjoying the show. He whispered to himself, "I hate to admit it, but this is the best fight I've ever seen." Then he shouted, "Come on Alex, quit playing with him, finish him." But even as he said it, he knew that it was going to be easier said than done.

Lara was down on his knees again winded. These two were beating the shit out of each other, but Tito had the best of Alex at this point.

Alex Lara reached for a bottle nearby and broke it, rushing Tito. Officer Lara yelled, "I'll cut your throat Tito, die motherfucker!"

Tito backpedaled and saw a trashcan lid. He dove for it and used it as a shield right on time as Lara swung the broken bottle tip, completely smashing to pieces. Lara had crushed his hand and was in pain. Tito backed up toward the cruiser. Shield in hand, looking like an ancient Aztec warrior.

Lara yelled at Yang, "Give me my Billy club!"

Tito said, "Oh we're doin it like that now? Fuck it! All's fair in love and war que no?"

Lara nodded yes. Yang put his pistol on the hood of the cruiser, reached over to the side of Lara's belt, pulled out his Billy club and threw it towards his partner.

That's all Tito needed was for Yang to lose focus on Lucky Tito. As he threw the billyclub, Tito saw his opportunity and quickly took it. He threw the trashcan lid at Yang and dove for Officer Yang's loaded gun. He captured his second chance with that move. Lucky Tito, in one swift motion, had Officer Yang by the hair, using him as a human shield.

Lara ran head down toward the back of the cruiser, reaching for his belt on the hood on the way but had no luck. He reached at his ankle 38 Revolver and pointed it at Tito and his partner Yang on the other side of the cruiser. Lara hollered, "Let him go Tito! Put the gun down now, right now!" Alex Lara looked around.

Lucky Tito had the gun to Officer Yang's head. He said, "Man Alex, you're fucking up. You're making me do this. I don't wanna have to smoke him. You let me go, that's how we fix this situation man!"

Lara said, "Fuck that! You're going to die in prison. Let my partner go!"

Officer Yang told his partner, "Just let him go Alex. We'll get him later."

Lara said, "No we'll get him now! He won't kill you. He don't got killer in him."

With that Officer Yang felt like his partner had abandoned him and was so caught up in his emotions that he told Tito, "Look, move to the right side of the cruiser. Our car camera is on. Don't shoot me. I'll confess to setting you up. Just let me go and run. Alex will throw his 38 and you take off. Just don't shoot me please, I have a family."

You see, Yang saw a part of Tito during the fight that showed him that if you push anybody too hard, they'll eventually push back. Put a cat and a dog in a corner and the cat will scratch the dog's eyes out!

Officer Lara yelled, "What the fuck are you saying Yang! Shut your mouth, we aren't confessing to shit! Tito's a scandalous dope fiend. They'll believe us over him! Whose side are you on?"

Officer Yang answered, "I'm on my side. He don't got a gun at *your* head!"

Lucky Tito placed him and his hostage in front of the cop car camera and whispered, "Speak your peace brother and tell it all." Tito took the gun from Yang's head and put it to Yang's back. Then he choked Yang from behind saying, "Spit it out, this is your last chance. I got nothing to lose!"

Officer Yang spoke, "There's a situation as you can see. Me and my partner Alex Lara set..."

Yang never finished his sentence.

Officer Lara hollered, "I told you to shut your mother fucking mouth!" Then Lara shot his partner Yang in his mouth, blowing bloody pieces of flesh and brain fragments all over Tito's face!

Tito lost his hostage and stood there shocked that Lara had killed his own partner. Tito looked around to escape.

There was an old white woman in her back yard observing the whole scene. She was unseen until Lucky Tito noticed her looking at him, scared as hell, biting her nails.

Officer Lara popped two hot shots at Tito's head, but just missed him. Lucky Tito ducked and ran to the right, popping shots right back at Officer Lara. Tito jumped onto the dumpster where the dead body was, and from there he hopped over the big grey brick wall, popping two more shots at Lara, who was shooting at Tito as well.

"Die Motherfucker!" Lara yelled, as he emptied his revolver's cylinder in Tito's direction.

Lucky Tito was living up to his name because not one of those killer bees hit him!

Lara ran and grabbed his police issued gloc and jumped on the trash dumpster, popping more rounds at Lucky Tito. He was only breaking windows and tearing up gravel. He whispered under his breath, "lucky bastard." The chase was on once again.

Officer Lara went to his cop cruiser and called for assistance. "Officer down! Suspect is Tito Lopez wanted for PC 187. Last seen running down 7th towards H. St."

Lara then slugged his cop car camera and it fell to the floor in the car. Officer Lara got his 38-pistol, dirty murder weapon, and threw it in the bushes to the left. The old woman was still there, but hiding behind a shed and she saw the 38 pistol land in her bushes.

Pastor Rick was standing outside waiting for Tito when he heard the gunshots going off in rapid succession. A second later, Lucky Tito Lopez was running past the church. He made eye contact with the pastor and yelled, "No! Go inside!"

Tito was full of blood and had a black gun in his hands, looking like a wild man, sprinting.

Pastor Rick yelled, "Come back Tito, I'll help you. Come back brother!"

Tito shook his head 'no' and increased his pace, and within three seconds he was out of sight. Pastor Rick made the sign of the cross and kissed his crucifix charm, then went into the church to take a knee and pray to God to help Tito. Something told Pastor Rick that Tito was past the point of no return though.

He heard sirens and went outside and saw Officer Lara speeding by toward Tito's direction. Pastor Rick knew this wouldn't end well. There had been bad blood between Alex Lara and Tito Lopez for years. But this time the law was on Alex's side as Tito ran back into insanity.

MVP-(MOST VALUABLE PLAYER)
PAST-DECEMBER 1ST, 1999

Baby Zoe-LaLa was no longer a baby. She was 16 years old and still living in a Correctional Placement Home for girls in the city of Mentone. She was three cities away from Colton, which she considered home. Zoe-LaLa still considered Denise her mom and Tito as her brother. Through the past 16 years, Denise and Tito were there as much as possible. They both sent Zoe-LaLa money every month, and packages of food, goodies, clothes, cd's and a cd player. They sent everything that she was allowed to have. It's as if LaLa had been doing time since the age of two. Once she turned 18, she'd be considered an adult and be released. She planned to go home with Denise and Tito, her only family.

Denise had filed the appropriate paperwork to adopt Zoe-LaLa when she was seven years old. Denise had her life on track by then, but the courts still denied Denise as a capable parent. The court's argument was that she was considered irresponsible, because when Tito had found baby Zoe, Denise hadn't turned her into Child Protective Services, which the courts deemed would have been the right thing to do. Then, to add insult to injury, the courts ordered a one hundred yard restraining order against Denise and ordered the correctional home not to allow Denise to visit with baby Zoe-LaLa anymore.

Denise broke down in court crying her heart out, distraught and frustrated. She loved Zoe and would die for her. She decided living for her was better and taking care of her was the best thing. No one else wanted to adopt her. Denise didn't understand the system. It was all bad for a few years. Denise still showed up to visit, but was denied every time. She then filed for visitation rights, appealing the adoption judge's orders. She was denied again. Ms. Brown was an older African American woman who was in charge of the girls at the placement home. She would speak for Zoe Lopez on her behalf in court and also speak in favor of allowing Denise and Tito to visit Zoe. Ms. Brown felt Zoe needed some family in her life to help her keep pushing through her circumstances. Ms. Brown's words were disregarded in court and she didn't agree with the judge's decision. He hurt Zoe by trying to hurt Denise.

Ms. Brown and Denise had built a good rapport when Denise used to visit Zoe as a baby her first seven years. You could even say they became low-key friends. After the last court date when Denise was denied visitation. Ms. Brown walked up to Denise in the hall and gave her a tissue to wipe her tears.

She whispered in Denise's ear, "Forget that judge's decision, you are Zoe's mom. There are ways to see your baby without coming to the correctional home. You just have to be willing to suffer the consequences if the judge finds out that you broke the restraining order. It's mandatory that you keep my name out of it. I'm not trying to lose my job. That judge was an asshole."

Denise felt hope once again. The loophole was this: every Thursday at 6 p.m., the girls were taken to the City of Redlands and allowed to have a little fun for two hours at the Public Community Center. They'd play pool, karams, basketball, handball, or take karate classes. Ms. Brown and one other staff member were the escorts. The girls played games and mingled with other kids and people in the community. Now, if Denise or Tito just so happened to be there at that time and had fun with Zoe and were able to sit and visit and Ms. Brown turned a blind eye, then no violation would be reported. Ms. Brown's staff member had no idea of the legal restraints, so nothing suspicious was occurring in his eyes.

Also, Zoe and a handful of the girls at the home played sports at a park in Redlands. Soccer and Softball games were played every weekend, and if Denise and Tito happened to be there, well, you see where I'm going with this. This was the only quality time they had with Zoe to keep and maintain close tightknit family ties. You can believe Denise and Tito were at those public spots at the designated times. Sometimes Tito would be loaded or on a mission, so he wouldn't show up, but he'd send his love to Zoe with his mom. Zoe missed him so much when he was sent to Youth Authority.

Poor Zoe Lopez, it was hard for her to accept growing up in a correctional home when she hadn't even committed a crime to be placed there. Several times, she tried to convince Denise into helping her escape from the park or the community center.

One time, Denise told Zoe, "We can't do that baby. If you run, they'll eventually catch up to you and we'll never be able to see each other. Ms. Brown set this up for us. I can't betray her. Just look at it like this sweetheart, there are times in our lives we'll be going through something terrible. Some sort of trial or tribulation that you'll hate going through, but when you get through it and later examine the situation, it was good for you. It made you stronger or wiser or taught you something. As long as you learn from it mija. God won't put more than you can handle on your shoulders, and if it's too heavy, dig deep for strength. Pray to God and Jesus for help. He's walking at your side."

Zoe put her head on her mom's shoulder, hugging her and saying, "You're right. I'll be patient. I will be 18 in two years and then I can go home. I'm getting all 'A's' at school. I'm even studying the law too so I can become a Paralegal when I'm old enough. Maybe I can help girls like me, out of situations like this. If I'm excellent, maybe I can even become a lawyer mom. Then I can get my brother out of his messes when he's in jail, ha-ha." They both laughed.

Ms. Brown tapped her watch and signaled, five minutes until they had to leave the Community Center. Then she went to round up the rest of the girls. Zoe was going to Redlands High School and had an off-campus lunch from 11 to 12 noon. She'd eat at Cuca's Mexican Restaurant every day. Denise had a lunch break at 11:30, so a couple times a week she'd go to Cuca's to eat lunch with Zoe.

Zoe asked, "Are we on for lunch tomorrow?"

"You know it," Denise answered.

They kissed, hugged and said their goodbyes. Zoe was actually pretty mature and was doing excellent for her circumstances. She hardly got into any trouble at the home. She'd been in a few fights over the years dealing with bully bitches with attitudes causing problems. They started it, but she ended it. Those karate classes at the Community Center came in handy. For the most part, she was a humble young lady. Denise told her how they'd found her and what type of man Erik was, and she knew of Tito's trial and tribulations. When she turned 13, Denise felt that she was mature enough to know where she came from and about everything that happened when she was a baby. All this seemed to push Zoe to the right path, whereas another juvenile might have used the bad news as an excuse to act out and ride the wrong path.

Zoe vowed not to end up an addict or a criminal, like many of the girls she lived with. Maybe Denise was right and God had put Zoe in this situation to grow stronger and see the bad life from the inside out. Then, when she was released, she'd live right and as good as she could. She was focused and motivated and had a plan for her life. She was determined to come up in the world. Denise and Tito's pep talks helped a lot because they kept it real all the time.

Zoe-LaLa sat in the back of the van, looking out the window at the clouds and full moon singing, "La la la la la la means I love you...."She was in Lala land, singing her favorite oldie as she thought of her family future.

STEALING BASES
PRESENT DAY, MAY 5TH, 2008-8:45 A.M.

Lucky Tito dipped into Rexall Drug Store two blocks up the way from the dead end alley. He was winded, sweaty, bloody, and as sick as a dog, fiending for a fix. All he needed was one shot of heroin to get him back to a normal mind frame. He was looking at medications while trying to look inconspicuous. His nerves were shot and he was shaking as he walked down the aisles, checking items on the shelf. He saw one of his childhood homies, Anthony, aka 'Lefty' from Eastside Colton, working behind the prescription drug counter. Lefty had escaped the gangster lifestyle and had just gotten a job in order to take care of his kids and family. There were two customers in line, so Tito got in line behind them as he kept looking through the windows, scoping out the parking lot for cops. All was clear. As he waited, Tito was thinking of a master plan.

He knew deep down though that this was his last day on the streets. He'd either get life in prison or be murdered by the corrupt cops. He was now playing the game with three strikes and he had everything to lose. He was thinking of his mother and LaLa and his kid Frankie and Tina. He had to see them one more time before he died or went to jail. He thought to himself, *I gotta get money for my family. I can't leave them without. It's ride or die.*

Anthony said, "Next, may I help you?"

Tito walked up to the counter and said, "What's up Lefty?" Tito wiped his face.

"Tito? Damn, homeboy, you look all bad! What's going on with you bro?" Anthony asked.

He noticed three cop cars speeding by and Tito ducking down and grabbing Chapstick and a baseball cap that read *Yellow Jackets*. They made eye contact again and since Lefty and Lucky had been on a couple of missions together when they were kids, Anthony knew the cops were hunting Lucky Tito just by his paranoid movements. The police radio was sounding off in Lucky's pocket so he quickly turned the volume down. The bastard was smart about snatching a radio on his way out of the alley. With any luck, this would give him a heads up as to where the cops were looking for him at and he'd be able to stay a few steps ahead of the corrupt pigs, backtrack and head in the opposite direction.

Lefty had love and respect for Tito. He actually took Lefty to Victory Outreach Church once, and that's when Lefty was "saved" and quit the game. Lucky however, continued playing the game. In a way, Lucky was responsible for helping Lefty change his evil ways.

Tito told Anthony, "Yeah, Yeah, Lefty, it's all bad. Alex's bitch ass set me up for two murders. He's on that hater shit." Lucky picked out and put on a maroon Yellow Jackets baseball t-shirt to match his cap and change his APB identity.

Anthony said, "Man what are you going to do brother?"

Tito threw his hands up in frustration, "I can't even think straight, I need a fix. What's crackin with some morphine pills or tramadol's or oxy's or something? Gimme a bottle and I'll get on track! I'm sick as fuck dawg help me."

Anthony looked over Tito's shoulder and said, "Man Tito, my manager's already looking over here concerned. I can't give you nothing. I got kids and a wife to feed and I don't want to get fired."

Tito looked over his shoulder and saw the manager staring straight at him so he waved at him nervously, hoping he wouldn't call the cops.

Lucky Tito said, "Come on Anthony, help me! I can't think straight. How do I get out of this? I'm sick and the pigs are trying to kill me. I don't want to end up like Bandit or Boxer, come on dawg."

Anthony whispered, "They want you for two murders dawg, what's a robbery added? I got my car keys in my top right pocket. It's the green Cadillac Escalade in the parking lot. Rob me, take the money and get a hella lot of pills in the back on the top shelf. Just leave my car in the alley by your house. I'll pick it up later. The cameras are on us so make it look good, hit me a few times and be on your way."

Lucky Tito smiled as a plan of escape unfolded in his mind. "Man, you still got it in you bro! I don't know why I didn't think of it first." He looked at the Bank of America across the street and said, "The bank's next. I'm going out with a bang, a straight spree."

The store manager came over asking Anthony, "Is there a problem Pagdaleo?" staring at Lucky suspiciously.

Lucky Tito pulled the gloc out and said, "Naw, no problem if you hand over the cash and pills and all car keys."

Lucky grabbed the manager by the collar and escorted him to the narcotic medication area. "Hurry up and get me all the morphine, tramadol's and Oxycotins," he ordered, shoving him.

Then he put the gun to Anthony's chest and ordered him, "And YOU give me your keys and money out the register and make it snappy before I start capping!"

Anthony played his part and winked at Tito.

Tito winked back yelling, "Which car's yours old man!" The old manager was trembling with fear. He gave Lucky Tito a full bag of pills and his wallet.

Anthony said, "I aint giving you my keys dude, you can kill me!"

The manager said, "Anthony what are you thinking, it's just a car give him your keys!"

Tito said, "That's right, and just for you putting up a fuss, I'm taking *your* ride and…" he hit Anthony in the stomach. Anthony buckled, playing his part perfectly, acting hurt.

He handed Tito his keys and the manger went to his side. "No more sir, you got the drugs and money, please leave," the manager said.

Lucky Tito looked at both workers and their ID's and read, "Mr. Carter you live at 1516 Yellow Jasmin Road in Big Bear, and Mr. Pagdaleo, you live at 310 'C' Street in Colton. If you call the cops any sooner than a hour after I'm gone, I'll have your families murdered. I have a photographic memory. I'm gone."

Tito calmly put the pistol in his pocket and walked out of the store. Anthony felt like laughing because he knew that Tito wasn't a killer and that he wouldn't hurt anyone's family.

As Tito walked out of the store, he held the door open for a young woman. She smiled saying, "Thank you, you're so polite."

Tito tipped his hat and said, "You're welcome."

He then jumped into Anthony's green Escalade, sped off across the street and went through a similar routine of robbing the Bank of America. He came up close to $100,000 there. The first thing he did was to put two fat stacks, about five-thousand dollars in Anthony's glove department as a reward for helping him out. Then he jumped on the freeway eastbound toward his house on Grand Terrace. He hoped Tina and Zoe would be there. He popped a handful of morphine and chased it down with Anthony's leftover Starbucks coffee he'd left in the cup holder as he looked in the rearview mirror to see if he was being followed. No one was on his tail. He knew Anthony wouldn't let his manager call the cops and report him for at least a hour. He'd play the family card.

Therefore, he had time to get a few things done quickly. He thought *they want to give me life; I'll earn it and give em a reason to give me life.* He mumbled *I hope you're still walking at my side Lord; cuz the devil's hunting me Lord.* He accelerated to 60 miles per hour as he felt the morphine give him chills and comfort.

GRAND SLAM HOMERUN
PRESENT DAY, MAY 5TH, 2008-10:21 A.M.

As soon as Zoe-LaLa turned 18, she was released from the group home and went to live with Denise, the woman she had always considered mom. Zoe had her act together. She graduated from high school at the top of her class, earning all A's. She took college courses in Law. She was chasing her dream of becoming a lawyer. She had a clever mind and a sharp tongue, which she needed to be excellent at her job. She was doing things one-step at a time. She was a great Paralegal, learning the ropes at a high power and successful law firm.

She had never used drugs in her life. She drank occasionally but never abused alcohol. She had money and a car, all legit, and she was living well. Not bad for a 25 year old born into hell. Zoe attended church every week and loved the Lord Jesus and God the Father and she followed the Holy Spirit as her spirit guide. She was balanced. Zoe requested the day off work to babysit her nephew, Tito's son, Frankie-Boy. She was lounging around on the black pleather couch playing video games with Frankie-Boy. Zoe had grown up to be real fine. She was wearing some tight white sweats and a red sports top that showed off every curve of her luscious figure. Her light brown streaked, wet, curly hair was in a ponytail. She was gorgeous without makeup, a straight dime-piece, top-notch woman.

Frankie-Boy was wearing blue jeans and a black and white WWE wrestling T-shirt. He was a hyper six-year old. He was focused on video games and didn't notice his pops, Tito, walking into the house until Aunt Zoe made him aware. Zoe noticed Tito's wounds and she got up to follow him to the restroom. But before she did, she messed up Frankie-Boy's hair and playfully knocked the game controller out of his hand saying, "You win F-boy. I have to talk to your Pops."

Frankie-Boy teased, "You're a cheater Tia. I would've whooped on you worser. You can't see me," he said, and then he put his hand over his eyes, waving it over his face, imitating his favorite wrestler, John Cana's, signature move. He hit reset on the game of Grand Theft Auto with no idea that in a few minutes he was about to be involved in a real-life GTA. Seeing his Pops he said, "Hi Pops, love you." Then he refocused on his game.

Zoe looked out the window and saw a green Escalade in the driveway. Then she walked in on Tito, who was washing up.

She asked, "What's up bro whose ride is that?"

She saw his face in the mirror. He was nervous and loaded. He reached down for the Rexall Drugstore bag full of pills and money. He then popped some more morphine and tramadol pills and drank from the faucet.

Zoe jokingly asked, "Damn, did you rob a bank? Whose money is that?" Her eyes were wide with curiosity.

Tito finally nodded and spoke, "Yeah I hit the Bank of America." He then explained the events that had occurred throughout the morning as quickly as possible. He asked, "Where's Tina? Why are you here?"

Zoe answered, "Man Alex is an ass! I'm babysitting your boy. Tina's with mom at Victory Outreach Church helping set up for the Cinco de Mayo fiesta. There's going to be Aztec dancers there this year. What are you going to do bro," she asked in a worried tone as she put Band-Aids on his wounds.

Tito reached into the bag and pulled out three stacks of hundred dollar bills and handed it to Zoe, then threw the pills and the rest of the money in a backpack.

Tito said, "Give this money to your boss. Explain what happened, except that this money is stolen from a bank. Tell him this is his retainer. I need a good lawyer who can battle in the courtroom. Then call internal affairs and ask for Ms. Ramirez. She investigated Officers Yang and Lara when they almost killed me and tried setting me up before. Tell her get the videotape from Alex's cop car; it'll prove Alex killed Yang, not me. Also, there's an old lady who saw Lara kill Yang. There's a dead black dude in the dumpster too. If you can tell Pastor Rick what happened… matter fact, here's two more racks of cash for bail money if I get caught." Tito handed Zoe cash. She was trying to take all this in and stay in step with the plan.

Tito was playing with life and death and one slip meant that he'd be dead. Zoe began crying as his reality sunk in.

Tito hugged his sister saying, "Come on LaLa shake it off, I'm still here. Let's beat Alex at his own game. Play your part and I'll play mine. I need to get in that fast lane and push hard. I'm taking Frankie-Boy to the church with mom and Tina. Please hurry, let's go!" He spanked Zoe on the booty, "Make it snappy girl, hustle hustle!"

Zoe thought about how Tito had always been there for her and saved her more than a few times. She snapped out of it, gathering her composure and wits and didn't even think twice about helping her brother Tito.

She said, "I got your back bro, I'll help you out of this shit Alex is dragging you through."

She threw the bundle of money in her purse, opened her cell phone and started calling phone numbers as she sped off in her gold Lexus ride. Time was of the essence. Tito put a couple of new syringes in his pocket, and in no time, he and his son were on the freeway heading toward San Bernardino Victory Outreach Church. Frankie-Boy was playing with the radio as they got off the freeway. When they passed a Chuck E Cheese Pizza place Frankie-Boy got excited, "Look Pops, Chuck E Cheese's! Let's go play games Yeah? Please…please, I love Chuck E Cheese."

Tito was weaving in and out of traffic, smashing sideways, looking in the side and rearview mirrors for cops. He said, "Not today Frankie-Boy, we're going to the church with Nana and Mama. There's game booths there today and rides too." Frankie-Boy folded his arms pissed off, wrinkling his nose at his Pops.

"Nah uh, there's no games at church. It's just God's house, they just pray there. There's no games."

Tito's heart skipped a beat and he pumped his brakes when he saw a San Bernardino cop in front of him coming his way in the opposite lane. He put his hand on Frankie-Boy and strapped on his seat belt.

"Sit down mijo. Stay in your seat belt or the cops will pull me over and take me to jail. Behave. Today's Cinco de Mayo so there's a carnival at the church, you'll see in a minute."

Tito decided to take the back streets to the church so he made a left turn. Just his luck the cop turned down the street right behind him, so Tito made a right turn going off track from his destination. He cruised the speed limit, trying not to give the cop a reason to pull him over but the cop was still on his tail.

Tito turned off the radio and told Frankie, "Behave, the cops are behind us."

Frankie looked back and flipped the cops off saying, "I don't like pigs Pops."

Luckily, the windows were tinted and they didn't see the rowdy kid. All of a sudden, Frankie-Boy jumped with excitement hollering, "Look Pops a park! A jungle gym and swings! Can we stop, please Pops?"

Tito was focused on his rearview mirror. Then he had an idea and pulled over at the park. Before he knew it, Frankie-Boy had jumped out and was running to the sandbox, kicking up dust. He sat on a swing, moving his legs back and forth happily, smiling away, unaware of the danger. Tito got out of the Escalade wearing his hat low. The cop cruised by slowly eyeing Tito, but didn't recognize him. He hit his brakes, but then apparently he got a call on his radio because he suddenly sped off. Tito jogged over to his son and pushed him on the swing.

Frankie-Boy squealed, "Higher Pops, higher!"

Tito had gotten lucky once again, the heat missed him. Every instinct within Tito was telling him to leave, to run. Then, to top things off, Lucky Tito was suddenly aware of his surroundings. He and his son were playing in enemy territory. He was at Westside 7th St. Placita Park. He had been shot about half a block down from there when he was a youngster, trying to pull a home invasion robbery. He didn't see any gangsters around and it was still early morning. The G's usually came out at night, so he decided they were safe for the most part. At least he was out of Colton and out of the cops' radar. He knew he had to get rid of Anthony's Escalade soon though. Frankie-Boy jumped off the swing and went to go work the jungle gym obstacles. He was hollering, "Look Pops! I did the web! I did the bars!"

Tito decided to sit on the bench, smoke and watch over the whole area and think of what to do next. He knew he had to give his son at least one more good time and a fun memory of them together. This might be his last day of freedom or even his last day on earth. He cheered his son on as he played, "You're a little monkey boy ain't you!"

Tito checked out traffic and people coming out of the store across the street. The playground was situated toward the back of the park, hidden from the street for the most part. He remembered coming to this same park as a kid with his father Erik, before Erik became an addict. Tito was tripping on how history had a way of repeating itself. All he knew was that he was a much better father to Frankie-Boy than Erik had been to him and he was proud of himself for that. He opened a pill bottle and chewed on some Oxycotins. The sickness was already ceasing and he felt all right. He was high again and could think clearly.

He looked down and opened the backpack, throwing the pill bottle back in it and zipping it up.

Some voices to his right got his attention. He saw two gangster cholos, most likely from 7th St coming out of the park restroom. Tito unlocked the safety on the gloc in his pocket. Tito focused on one particular gangster, a vet who looked and sounded familiar. He was about 45 or 50 years old, had dark brown skin and was bald. He had a long, grey, walrus-looking mustache and was tatted from head to toe. He was wearing a brown Khaki suit. The other gangster wore all black. He was real young, maybe 15 or 16 years old. He was wiping away blood off his bicep, walking sideways and off balance. Tito recognized the symptoms. The kid had just slammed some heroin and was in a zombie state of mind. Tito just eyed the two enemies from a distance while also looking at his son.

The veteran slapped the youngster on the back of the head saying, "Come on, put some pep in your step lil foolio. You control the high, don't let it control you. The first high is free, the second will cost you your soul." The veteran laughed at his own joke.

The young G wiped the sweat off his forehead and scratched at his arms saying, "Yeah Yeah ese, I'm commin. Kick back, don't be smackin me ese. I don't play that shit!"

The veteran G smacked the youngster again saying, "Shut up, you'll play what I tell you to play lil fucker. Your soul's mine. You don't even know it. The golden road to heaven starts in hell and it's a long road idiot."

Those words from the veterano triggered a memory in Tito. *The golden road to heaven starts in hell…,* his father Erik used to say those same words regularly. Then it all came to Tito. He mumbled, *Veneno,* which means venom or poison. Veneno was the name of the vet gangster who got Tito's father hooked on heroin. The name fit the vet too. All he did was spread poison as a dope dealer. Lucky Tito and Veneno made eye contact and Veneno spit like a snake and gave Tito a dirty look. Tito thought, *Yeah, it's definitely Veneno. He's older but there goes his tattoo horns on his forehead.* He'd heard Veneno got 25 years to life a few years back. I guess you can't believe everything you hear because here he was live and in the flesh. When he was a youngster, robbing connections in San Bernardino, Lucky Tito's whole motivation had been to catch Veneno slipping and kill him.

Tito instinctively put his hand in his pocket and tapped the glocs trigger, desperately wanting to shoot Veneno's cocky ass. Hate pumped through Lucky Tito's heart and veins. It was kind of ironic that Lucky wanted to punish Veneno for hooking his father and ruining his family life, yet on the other hand, as Lucky saw the youngster scratching from the euphoria of the heroin, he craved a shot of heroin at the same time. He kept his cool for Frankie-Boy's sake.

Frankie-Boy shouted, "Look Pops, I'm skipping two bars at a time!"

Tito smiled and yelled to his son, "Yeah you're a gorilla. You got skills mijo."

Frankie-Boy jumped down scratching his armpits and pouncing around, imitating a gorilla, making monkey sounds.

"Ewe, ewe, ah-ah. G-unit, Gorilla unit huh Pops?"

Tito laughed half-heartedly, but watched Veneno with his peripheral vision. He desperately wanted to fuck off Veneno's world. He was on the run and he had nothing to lose… except his son was with him. So he started thinking of a plan to have his cake and eat it too by erasing Veneno off the map. Right then two Jehovah Witnesses walked through the park. They were wearing brown matching suits with white shirts and black ties, Bibles in hand.

One man addressed Tito extending his hand out to shake he said, "Hello sir. I'm Brother Darren and this is Brother David. We're Jehovah Witnesses. I'm wondering if we can share the truth with you about Jehovah God."

Tito's eyes were on Veneno, who flicked his cigarette and walked out of the park, heading down 7th St.

Tito shook the man's hand and said, "Yes you can share the truth, but only if you do me a favor and watch my son for a few minutes while I go to the store across the street real quick. I'll donate one, two, three, hundred dollars to your church or Kingdom Hall if you will."

He grabbed a handful of money from the backpack and gave it to one of the startled Jehovah Witnesses who said, "Okay, I guess that'll be alright."

Tito hollered at his son, "Frankie-Boy, these Christian dudes are going to watch you for a quick minute, I'm going to the store."

Frankie-Boy was at the top of the slide and hollered, "Ok Pops buy me a Orange Crush and cheese popcorn," as he slid to the bottom and ran back up.

The two men went to the sandbox to talk to Frankie-Boy, watching him closely as Tito took off jogging across the park. The two Jehovah Witnesses didn't even notice that Tito didn't go to the store. He made a right on 7th St., trailing Veneno's route.

Tito slowed his roll on 7th St. because he saw Veneno standing in front of a house up the block with his arm around a chola gangster chick. Tito watched as Veneno slid her a sack of dope and she casually put the money in his pocket. Another chola was on the porch of the reddish brick house when Veneno escorted her into the house.

Lucky Tito crept up the stairs and onto the porch and looked inside the window and saw the chick on her knees and Veneno unzipping his pants about to get a blowjob.

Tito thought, P*erfect I'll catch him with his pants down.*

Tito turned the doorknob slowly but it was locked so He made a decision to get in the house so he played the customer roll and he knocked on the door three times.

Tito heard Veneno inside cursing. "Fuck man I can't even get my fuckin dick sucked in peace who the fuck is it?"

Veneno looked out the window and saw Tito flashing a couple hundred-dollar bills smiling all friendly.

"I need some black man, the homie said you got the bomb shit and I got money to spend," Tito told him.

Veneno's greed watered his mouth as his eyes went *ching, ching, like d*ollar signs.

He zipped up his pants and told the chick behind him, "Wait a minute, it's MOB on mines."

She asked, "What's that mean?"

Veneno snickered, "M-O-B stupid. Money over Bitches, I gotta make a sale." Veneno opened the door saying, "Who the fuck are you, do I know you? Which homie told you I got smack?"

Lucky Tito pulled out his, or you could say Officer Yang's, 9 mil Gloc and put it to Veneno's forehead saying, "Shut the fuck up and move backwards into the pad and lift your hands too."

The chick tried crawling away whimpering, "Oh my God don't hurt me."

Tito said, "Don't move-freeze bitch!" Lucky Tito pistol-whipped Veneno two times, dropping him to his back.

Veneno tried acting brave, even though he was dazed. He said "What the fuck ese, do you know who you're fuckin with, do you know who I am puto?"

Lucky Tito kicked his teeth in until his mouth was full of blood, Lucky Tito said, "I got your puto right here! I don't give a fuck who you think you are, Mafia or not I got beef and you're gonna get a taste of your own medicine PUTO!" Tito mocked.

The chick was scared out of her wits and moved away from Veneno. Lucky Tito pulled out a blue bandana and ordered the chick to tie Veneno's hands behind his back and force him onto his stomach.

Veneno threatened her, "Don't touch me bitch or I'll kill you."

She backed up but then Tito threatened, "I'll kill you if you don't do it, and he aint killin no one ever again."

Lucky Tito shot Veneno in his kneecaps, both of them, to show them he wasn't playing games. Veneno was screaming in pain like a punk ass bitch. All that acting hard and playing the brave heart roll went out the window as he was tied up in seconds.

Lucky Tito ordered the chick to get in Veneno's pockets and cook up the heroin. He threw her two syringes and told her, "Fill em both up, thick, thick, killer shit."

As she did that Lucky Tito introduced himself and told Veneno where he'd gone wrong by getting Erik addicted to dope.

Veneno's ego and pride pushed him to spit blood at Lucky Tito and he screamed, "Fuck your Pops and your family, I don't give a fuck about none of them ese! They can all die, it aint my first or my last ese!"

Lucky Tito laughed and put the gun in Veneno's bloody mouth saying, "That's where you're wrong. It was and is your last sucker!" Tito hollered, "Die!" and shoved the gun down Veneno's throat, choking him and acting like he was going to pull the trigger.

Veneno's eyes popped out of his sockets because he was filled with fear now as Lucky Tito stood over him, provoking him, knowing damn well that he had all the power.

He said, "It's funny how you fell into my lap after all these years. Now we're going to have a going away party for ol' Veneno, the one who poisons the barrio." Tito motioned for the chick to stick Veneno in the arm with the heroin.

The chick asked, "Is the other one for you or me? I need a fix too. He was going to give me one if I sucked…"

Lucky waved the gun gesturing, 'no' and thinking, *this dumb bitch don't get what's happening yet, all she cares about is a fix-a-shot.*

Tito said, "They're both for Veneno, you can have his money and the rest of the heroin after I leave. He won't need it no more."

The chick said, "If I shoot him up with both syringes he'll overdose and die," as if Tito didn't know that.

Tito put the gun to his own temple nodding and said, "Yes, finally you get it chica, now shootem up ASAP. I'm in a hurry." Tito looked at his watch and saw that he'd been gone eight minutes already.

Veneno hollered, "Fuck you ese, fuck your life!" as he slipped into darkness, slipped into the fiery pits of hell.

Lucky Tito told Veneno, "That's the thing fool-you fucked my life up so now I take yours! What's fair is fair."

The chick right away began cooking a shot up for herself like an eager fiend. Lucky Tito wanted a fix too but the pills were holding him down.

There was a knock at the door and Tito jumped and spun around. Looking out the peep hole he saw that a black hustler type looking guy and a white chick were standing there banging on the door, hollering, "Come on Veneno, I got places to be cuz. It's 8-Ball my nigga. I got fat chunks of that tar nigga open up. I gotta drop and get ghost."

8-Ball was paranoid. Being a professional dope man, he always expected a jack move, especially when dealing with Mexicans, which he tried not to do too often. But the Mexicans loved the heroin and had the money. He'd been working with Veneno for the past year, balling out of control. At the same time, his dope was slowly poisoning his enemies, Westside 7th Street Verdugo, who were at war with the Westside projects and 8-Ball's hood and gang. 8-Ball held a blue duffle bag and was knocking impatiently.

Lucky Tito thought, *I might've got lucky and hit the jackpot. I hope there are a few kilos in that duffle bag.*

Lucky Tito dragged Veneno's dead body into the hall and ordered the chick into the room out of sight.

Lucky Tito opened the door with a smile and said, "Come on in 8-Ball, Veneno's taking a shit. He'll be out in a minute."

8-Ball pushed his blonde broad in the house and asked Tito, "Who is you cuz? Veneno knows the rules, no otha essays in the crib when I be here." 8-Ball looked up and down at Tito suspiciously.

All of a sudden, the blonde broad passed the hall and saw Veneno's dead body and she screamed. 8-Ball didn't hesitate, he swung the bag at Lucky Tito who caught it and hooked his hand around it and yanked it, pulling out his black gloc in one swift motion. 8-Ball quickly took off like a greyhound sprinting out the door and up the street, looking back but not stopping.

Lucky Tito went up to 8-Ball's blonde broad in the house and pointed the gun at her saying, "Tell me you got the keys to that white Avalanche truck."

She nodded yes, and pulled them out of her purse and handed them to Lucky Tito saying, "Take it just don't hurt me."

Lucky Tito said, "Your old man left you for dead, what's up with that? Go in that room and don't come out."

He checked his watch and ran out with a duffle bag full of heroin. How can a man get so lucky? He had his backpack full of money and pills and he had a new truck.

He peeled out and pulled a U-turn, driving up into the park stopping at the sandbox. He opened the door yelling, "Get in Frankie, let's go!"

His son ran and jumped in saying, "Where's my soda and popcorn? Whose car is this Pops?" The kid was playing real life Grand Theft Auto.

Lucky Tito answered, "They didn't have any, and it's my friend's."

He then threw a couple hundred more dollars out of the window at the Jehovah Witnesses, whose mouths were hanging wide open and said, "God bless you both, thank you," and he sped off down the street.

Lucky Tito was back on track speeding off towards Victory Outreach Church to drop off Frankie-Boy with Tina and his mom Denise. Tito had put down the hit in less than 15 minutes. *Not bad, he thought as he* felt an adrenaline rush.

When he turned on the ignition, a CD that 8-ball had been listening to, started playing and the lyrics seemed to match with what Tito was going through.

The rapper "Redrum" spit the lyrics,
'I'm in this game too deep…
I can't sleep cuz police creep.
And gotta APB on me.
They want me six feet…
I'm slipping into a world of insanity.
I feel demons attacking me.
But I know God's walking with a G…
I'm terrorizing these empire streets…
When all I want is peace.'

Lucky Tito turned up the volume of the song on the slammin system and as Frankie-Boy danced along in the front seat, they both bobbed their heads to the music.

TAKING ONE FOR THE TEAM
PRESENT DAY, MAY 5TH, 2008-11:05 A.M.

Officer Lara was furious and losing control, talking to himself like a J-cat as he hunted for Tito. *He's got to die. No ifs ands or buts about it, he's going to die. Dumb bitch-he has Yang's gun, he mumbled.* "Fuck Yang! Fuck, fuck, fuck!" he yelled hitting on the steering wheel in frustration.

Lara had already hit one known dope spot Lucky Tito scored from. He crept through every back street and stalked through every alley. Nothing! He even went as far as going to Lucky Tito's house in Grand Terrace kicking in the door and ransacking the pad. All dead ends. He secretly hoped he saw Tina there. He still loved her after all these years. He couldn't shake it.

Sargent Garza kept calling Lara over the cop radio, but Alex Lara ignored his boss's attempts to reach him. He threw his shoulder radio on the floor of the passenger seat next to the broken cop cruiser camera. He thought he'd erase all incriminating evidence on the cop camera. Everything isn't always what you think though.

Lara got an idea. He was going to double back toward the alley where Yang and Crip boy were lying dead. He heard there were two robberies in the vicinity soon after Lucky Tito had run off. He'd go ask questions at the Rexall Drug Store and see if Tito was stupid enough to pull off those robberies. He didn't think Tito was that stupid to add wood to the fire, but on second thought, he knew Tito was that desperate to get away and he'd need money and a ride.

When he drove up there were cop cars at the Bank of America and two cops interviewing two witnesses outside the Rexall Drug Store. He pulled into the parking lot of the Rexall Drug store first.

Lara instantly recognized Anthony Pagdaleo a.k.a. Lefty, as one of the witnesses being interviewed. Lefty was well known as one of Lucky's road dogs from back in the day. Lara got out of his cruiser evilly grinning as he and Anthony made eye contact. If looks could kill Anthony would be dead. Lara looked psychotic, like he was spun out on crystal meth. He was sweating puddles, leaking blood. He rotated his neck, cracking it and cracking his knuckles as if he was getting ready for a fight.

Seeing him, Anthony felt trouble brewing and felt butterflies flying through his stomach as he thought, *Man this might not go down as smooth as I thought, I'm going to have to take one for the team.* Anthony took a deep breath and stepped up to the plate as Alex Lara walked up into his face, hella loked out.

Sargent Garza was hella pissed with a whole lot on his plate and it wasn't even noon yet. Although Sargent Garza had his trained officers all around, he heard them asking a lot of questions but getting no answers back. All he heard were excuses. The raid had gone sour. The tipster said that there would be two kilos of heroin in Redrum's house, but all they'd found was 30 grams. The aftermath was all-bad. Three officers and one suspect had been shot, one officer had been chewed up and mauled by a vicious pit bull and the other three suspects had escaped. All this for only 30 grams was not worth the hassle.

Then, to add insult to injury, Sgt. Garza had a bone to pick with Officer Lara because in the middle of Garza's drug raid, he'd gotten a call from Ms. Ramirez of Internal Affairs, ordering Sgt. Garza to relieve Officer Lara of his duties pending investigation. Sgt. Garza wasn't trying to hear some bitch give him strict orders while he was working!

He was pissed that Officer Lara wasn't answering or returning his radio calls and what really made Sgt. Garza's blood boil was that Officer Lara had not even waited for the ambulance or backup to show up in that alley. He'd just left his partner Yang's dead body laid out and abandoned.

Sgt. Garza knew in his heart that something wasn't right and that Lara had most likely just hung his self, committing career suicide. Word was out that Tito Lopez had something to do with two murders and two robberies in Colton and one murder and robbery in San Bernardino. All these crimes could be filed as possible death penalty cases. Sgt. Garza had his right-hand man finish up the investigation at the drug raid while he spoke with the head of the San Bernardino

Homicide Detectives and was allowed to intervene and bring as much help and info to the crime scene at 7th St. and L St. on the Westside.

Chica actually remembered and gave the cops Tito Lopez's name. Sgt. Garza brought a photo lineup with Tito's picture in it. 8-Ball, two Jehovah Witnesses, the blonde broad Marlene, and Chica, whose real name was Teresa, all picked out Tito's picture.

Sgt. Garza whistled and told the homicide detectives, "The prime suspect is Tito Lucky Lopez. He's a North Colton gang member, about 38 years old or so. This is out of character and not his usual M-O. He's just a dope fiend and has mostly been arrested for petty thefts, nothing too serious."

San Bernardino detective Johnson interrupted saying, "Murder and robbery is pretty serious in San Bernardino, Sgt. Garza. If it's no big deal in Colton, we'll just handle this case ourselves." Sgt. Garza pulled out a cigarette and lit up.

"You misunderstood me, murder and robberies are dead serious to CPD, literally. What I'm saying is that I think one of my officers, 'Lara' pushed Tito over the edge or tried setting him up."

The SBPD Detective replied, "I don't know about all that, all I know is that I've got five witnesses here who say Tito Lopez committed a murder robbery in my city, and it wasn't a set-up. If it walks like a duck and talks like a duck…"

Sgt. Garza finished his sentence, "Then it's a duck, Yeah, Yeah, I understand all that."

Sgt. Garza saw that he wasn't going to get anywhere with these two detectives because quiet as kept, these two police departments were rivals, you could say, just as the Colton and San Bernardino gangs didn't get along.

8-Ball told the cops that Tito jacked his money and his truck, but didn't mention the dope. Then 8-Ball told Sgt. Garza and the SBPD detectives, "My cell phones in da glove compartment of da Avalanche. It has a navigation tracer chip in it, and maybe y'all can find dat foo like dat?"

Sgt. Garza didn't hesitate to make a call, run a make, and then jump in the fast lane. He found out that the Avalanche was in San Bernardino, moving east on Mill St. Six cops followed him on the hunt for a possible cop killer on a vicious spree. They sped off with lights on but sirens off. They wanted the element of surprise on their side.

Denise and Tina were at the church blowing up balloons when LaLa called Tina.

She asked, "Has Tito and Frankie-Boy gotten there yet?"

Tina answered, "No, why would they be coming here, what happened LaLa?"

Zoe-LaLa took a deep breath and told Tina about everything that had been happening all morning.

Her last sentence was, "Tell Tito Ms. Ramirez suggests that he turn himself in at her office. Here's her phone number, please give it to him."

Tina tearfully jotted down the phone number and said, "Thank you mija, I'll tell him."

After they'd hung up, Denise walked up looking worried and asking, "What's wrong mija, why are you crying Tina?"

Tina was sad and disturbed because she couldn't believe what she'd just heard. She repeated the run down to Denise who hugged her. They both began praying together, crying their hearts out to the Lord.

Frankie-Boy was searching the glove compartment when Lucky Tito pulled up to the Victory Outreach Church parking lot.

Frankie-Boy asked, "Hey Pops, there's change and markers in here and all kinds of good stuff. Can I have them Pops?"

Tito was distracted, searching the crowded fiesta. He saw Tina and his mom and he said, "Yeah boy, you can have whatever's in there. Let's go though, put that junk in your pocket."

He opened the door and went to the passenger side where Frankie-Boy was happily stuffing his pockets. Tito grabbed his son's hand and casually strolled through the aisles of food and game booths.

Frankie-Boy excitedly said, "Look Pops, let's stop here. Can I get on that ride, huh Pops can I?"

Frankie-Boy saw his mother Tina and ran to them. Both Denise and Tina looked distraught so Tito knew that they'd already caught wind of the whole ordeal. Frankie-Boy hugged his mom then grabbed his Nana Denise's hand and said, "Come on Nana, take me to the rides."

Denise gave her grandson a soda, an ice cream and some ride tickets, all the while staring at Tito with one raised eyebrow. She knew Tito was in deep, deep trouble this time. He put his head down in shame and Denise and Tina both hugged him.

He whispered sadly, "It's not my fault. I didn't do shit. Alex set me up for double murder, so I jumped off the edge, head first into deep water to get money so you're all taken care of while I'm away."

He reached into the backpack, pulled out fat stacks of money and shoved it in Tina and his mom's hands.

Denise just froze and she felt a sharp pain her heart as she worried, thinking of how he could have gotten ahold of that much money.

He put two stacks back in the pack saying, "That should hold you down for a while, I did what I could babe, I'll send you more when it cools down. I'm heading out of state and then I'll reach you when the time is right. I might get a little ranch in Mexico and send for you but I gotta go now. I love you all! Pray for me. Oh Yeah, I got saved today with Pastor Rick, but then all hell broke loose… it's crazy."

Tina was holding Tito's hand and said, "I hate Alex's guts! LaLa said that Ms. Ramirez wants you to turn yourself in at her office, here's her cell number, she said to call her Tito," she said, handing him a slip of paper.

When she gave him the slip of paper, Tito put it in his pocket but waved off the idea of turning himself in.

"I don't think so, I'm running and this mess is too thick and sick!" he said.

Tears leaked from their eyes as Denise and Tina hugged Tito tightly as if it was the last time they'd see one another.

Frankie-Boy hugged their legs and said, "Group hug, group hug!" Then he noticed that everyone was crying so he asked, "Why is everyone crying, this is a carnival. You guys should be happy not sad. It's fun time!"

Tito picked up his son and hugged him and kissed his cheek telling him, "Frankie-Boy, I gotta leave for a while mijo, but I want you always to remember who loves you."

Frankie-Boy replied, "You love me like I love you right Pops? Where are you going, I want to go with you."

Lucky Tito heard the cop radio crackling in his pocket and heard that the cops were on the way to the church looking for him so he told his son and Tina, "You can't go with me-you need to take care of your moms for me. I love you mijo. Tina, put the money away in your purses and then go stash them both somewhere. Don't let them find the money, they're coming!"

He kissed his wife, son and mother and sprinted across the parking lot. He got ghost to Redlands. He knew he could lay low at his old stand by sancha's pad until he decided what to do next. He'd get high, maybe have sex and see what Ester's fine ass had in mind to help him concoct a master escape plan. She was actually pretty smart for an addict.

The sirens echoed in Tito's ears and lights flashed the car on the side of him as he jumped on the 215 freeway southbound, then the 10 freeway eastbound, heading towards Redlands, pedal to the metal.

He'd lucked out again. He kept rolling the dice with his life, praying he didn't crap out or hit snake eyes.

TIME OUT-MEETING ON THE MOUND
PRESENT DAY, MAY 5TH, 2008-1:15 P.M.

The crooked cop, Lara, pulled Anthony to the side of the Rexall Drug Store, hidden out of sight, and took over the questioning.

Lara was being aggressive with Anthony. "Look you little fuck head, you tell me where Tito went or I'll expose your gangbanger past to your boss and you'll lose your fucking job Lefty," he said tauntingly, pointing his finger in Anthony's chest. Lara just knew they were in cahoots.

Anthony shrugged. "I don't know nothing man, the dude robbed us and that's all I know. I ain't seen Tito in years man."

Lara slapped Anthony, who just took it with a smile saying, "You'll never find him before he exposes you. That's all I gotta say. Oh Yeah, wait til the homies get your ass in the joint. You're a done dotta pig! Ha-ha."

Lara slugged Anthony in the stomach and walked away frustrated. He knew Anthony had taken one for the team and wasn't going to spit out any info. He was baffled so he went across the street to the bank to ask questions, but he had no luck there either. All he had was dead ends.

Officer Luna tapped Lara on his shoulder saying, "Hey bro, the Sarge has been calling you. Do you have your hip radio with you?"

Lara threw his hands up disgustedly and answered, "No, that piece of shit Tito stole it. He's going to pay for killing my partner, I swear to God he'll pay!"

Officer Luna sympathized with Lara, giving him a brotherly hug saying, "We'll get him and send him straight to Death Row bro. Call the Sarge, He might have some new info, or other leads for you. I know he's on his tail. We just found out that Tito killed someone in San Bernardino."

Lara excitedly said, "Man why didn't you say that from the gate!"

Lara thought, *if I don't find Tito first I'll be the one on Death Row. Where's this son of a bitch hiding? He's got an instant death sentence coming. I'm done playing games.*

Officer Lara called his boss Sgt. Garza, who wasn't in a good mood at all. Lara sat in his cruiser and slammed the door, feeling pissed off as Garza chewed him out. But Lara managed to get the info he needed. Tito was at the church and there was a perimeter surrounding the Victory Outreach Carnival. The kids had a half day of school, so they were all swarming the Cinco de Mayo carnival across the street.

Lara disregarded his boss's orders to stand down and go to the Colton Police Department and start the police reports concerning the mornings' incidents. Lara was like a bloodhound hunting a criminal. His corrupt mind had his own plans brewing and there was nothing legal or nice about them.

On the way to the carnival, Lara made a quick stop at the wash in the Flats and let off two shots in the sand. He then gathered the shells and put a throwaway 22 pistol in between the hard, plastic back seat of his police cruiser and threw the shells on the narrow, back seat floor.

His plan was to take Tito into custody, but cuff his hands in the front. He knew that he would have a parade of cop cars following him, and that since Yang was his partner, he had the right to escort Tito to the station.

But Tito would never make it there alive. Lara would swerve in his cruiser, pull out his pistol and have the green light to smoke Tito.

Then he would quickly pull out and put the hidden 22 within Tito's reach. It would seem like someone slipped during the search and didn't find the 22 on Tito.

It would be their bad and then Lara would be the hero. He had it all planned out, stupid motherfucker!

Since Victory Outreach Church was in Verdugo Flats gang territory, San Bernardino's jurisdiction, SBPD moved in first with Colton PD following right behind them as back up.

The kids were everywhere, playing games, getting on rides, screaming and yelling, laughing and cheering.

The officers didn't want to stir the pot and get anybody hurt, so they patrolled the area with their guns holstered, but of course their hands were on the gun's grip, ready to draw down at the first sign of any problems or resistance.

When they arrived, Sgt. Garza immediately began questioning Pastor Thomas. 8-Ball's Avalanche truck wasn't in the parking lot, but his phone signal lead straight to the church and was still active. Maybe Tito was hiding close by.

Pastor Thomas pointed to a game booth saying, "That's Ms. Lopez over there. Maybe she's seen her son."

Sgt. Garza was on the phone with the cell phone tracking company and they insisted that the phone was within 30 feet of where he stood.

The smell of popcorn, cotton candy and Mexican food was in the air. The Zipper Ride cages were spinning crazily as people screamed from above. All that screaming had Sgt. Garza on edge. He thought the worst-people were screaming because Tito was doing dirt. He had to get himself together. Twelve officers were cautiously searching the premises.

Sgt. Garza stopped at Denise's booth where a little kid was throwing darts at a wall of rainbow colored balloons.

The kid cheered, "Hell Yeah, that's two! I got eight more to pop and that water gun prize is all me."

Denise Lopez suspiciously eyed Sgt. Garza thinking, *I know he doesn't think I'm giving him any info on my son.*

Sgt. Garza said, "Ms. Lopez can..."

She cut him off saying, "He's not here so why don't you all leave. You're ruining the kids' carnival. Go play cops and robbers on the streets."

Sgt. Garza asked, "Where is he then? This has to end peacefully. I don't want Tito to end up hurt or dead over a misunderstanding." His eyes searched the booths and parking lot as he spoke.

Denise smirked and tightened up her braid, adjusting her 'Jesus Loves You' t-shirt. She said, "Tito's already hurt. All you got to understand is that your crooked Officer Alex Lara hates my son and set him up!"

Sgt. Garza gave Denise a doubtful look, scratching his nose asking, "Is that what Tito told you?" Denise ignored his question and Garza asked, "Do you really believe that? You know when people chase the Dragon they do things out of character. Chasing heroin is committing slow suicide. You know, I can arrest you if you know where he's at and refuse to give me the info. That's considered obstructing justice and harboring a wanted fugitive!"

Denise gave free tickets to the kids at her booth and told them to go play another game somewhere else. As they left Frankie-Boy, her grandson, came running up to her.

She told Garza, "Look, I don't know where he is, and even if I did, I wouldn't tell you. Colton PD is more corrupt than L.A.'s Rampart Division. You're on your own, now leave me alone!"

Frankie-Boy yelled, "Nana, Nana I almost threw up on the ride, it was fun! I need a soda; can I have some more money? My Pops only let me have change and I threw all the quarters I had on the ashtray game."

Sgt. Garza looked down at Frankie-Boy as Denise pulled him to her side protectively.

Sgt. Garza asked Frankie, "Is Tito Lopez your dad?"

Frankie-Boy nodded, 'yes' but Denise snapped at Sgt. Garza saying, "Don't be asking my grandson any questions. You have your nerve!"

As he stood there, Sgt. Garza was still communicating with the tracking company and they told him the signal showed that the phone was right in front of him. He didn't see Tito around but finally, it hit Sgt. Garza and he asked, "Frankie do you have a phone in your pockets?"

Frankie-Boy looked up at his Nana Denise with a guilty look on his face and put his hands in his pockets.

Denise pulled him closer to her and told Sgt. Garza, "I told you not to ask him questions. Quit harassing my family and just leave us alone! We don't know where Tito's at. Leave, you're ruining the carnival!"

Sgt. Garza loudly and with authority responded, "Look Ms. Lopez, I'm not trying to be disrespectful or ruin anything but I've got a job to do. So either you check Frankie's pockets or I will check them. The phone is stolen property. Tito stole it from a white truck earlier today."

Frankie-Boy laughed and snickered at Sgt. Garza saying, "Naw uh, Pops didn't steal the truck, it's his friends, he let him use it. Pops said I can have his phone."

Then Frankie pulled it out and showed it to Sgt. Garza, but he turned his back on the cop saying, "And you can't use my phone, I don't like pigs." Frankie-Boy then gave Sgt. Garza the middle finger and said, "F-U-PIG!"

Denise held in a laugh because Frankie-Boy said exactly what Denise felt like saying, but she reached over, slapped his hand down and said, "Shhh…don't be disrespectful, give me the phone. I'll buy you a better one mijito. You gotta give him this one." She handed the phone over and said, "There, your mystery is solved, unless you're going to take a six-year old to Juvenile Hall." She put her hands on her hips and smirked at Sgt. Garza, who shook his head, no. She said,

"That's what I thought, now leave us alone!"

Sgt. Garza said, "I suggest you pray for Tito Ms. Lopez." He nodded respectfully at her, then turned around and waved the twelve-man team back to their squad cars as he spoke into the radio giving his higher-ups the bad news. "We've lost track of Tito Lopez. He got lucky again, but his luck's bound to run out sooner or later," he reported.

PLAYING HARDBALL
PRESENT DAY, MAY 5TH, 2008-2:05 P.M.

Instead of heading to Ester's pad in Redlands, Tito decided to head to a park up in the Loma Linda Hills overlooking the Inland Empire. It was a quiet spot, kind of hidden in the hills. People sometimes went to this park to make out at night. Nobody else was around as Tito sat there looking out over the cities of Colton, Loma Linda, San Bernardino and Redlands.

He searched for the flashing cop car lights of those crooked cops who were hunting for him. He felt at peace though, but knew it wouldn't last long because he had to keep pushing hard in the fast lane. He killed two hours doing inventory as he sat there counting money, checking out all his pills and chipping away at his brick of heroin. He guessed it was at least a kilo, maybe even two. Tito had everything he needed to make a clean getaway. He slammed a shot of heroin and felt lovely all over. He wasn't even paranoid or spooked because the cops were on his tail. He had the *'fuck it' attitude, like… whatever happens, happens, I'm going out with a bang.*

Tito drove to the city of Redlands and slowly cruised by the green house on the corner of Sun and Alta. He paused at the stop sign and turned up the music as loud as it would go, trying to get Ester's attention and see if she was home. The bass was subbin hella gangsta as lyrics by the rapper "Redrum" flowed,

'I got these freaks on the team…
So fine, something sexy out of your wet dreams…
Fantasies down to set you up for Benjamin Greens…
This G got a million scams and schemes…
Whatcha see aint necessarily what it seems…

Their curves got you hypnotized, settin you up for this G.'

Tito noticed that somebody looked out through the window blinds of Ester's house, so he turned the music down and spun two laps around the block to see if any cops were in the area. All was clear so he parked in the neighbor's garage, because there were two houses connected by the two garages and if the cops rolled up they'd think Tito was in the other house, not Esters.

Ester and Angela, her roommate, pretty much let all the Northside Redlands gangsters kick back and party at their pad. It was the chill spot, but kind of hot, because Redlands PD knew gang members posted there on a regular basis. They had raided the spot a few times already.

Tito knocked on the door and V-Capone from Northside Redlands opened the door. Tito walked in shaking his hand and giving V-Capone a homie love hug and asking, "Alright now dawg, what's it lookin like V-Capps?"

V-Capone answered, "Ah, you know, same ol shit. Posted up and heated."

Tito noticed the pistol in V-Capone's waistband. Tito also noticed there were two other gangsters and Angela in the kitchen smoking crystal out of a glass pipe. Both G's were strapped up too. He recognized Toker, but didn't know the other fool, who was mad-dogging him. He later found out that the fool's name was 'Jacker', from Varrio Redlands.

Northside Redlands and Varrio Redlands were enemies, but Jacker was Angela's brother and V-Capone was Ester's brother so their pad was a neutral zone, at least for Jacker. Besides, V-Capone and Toker were just smoking up all Jackers dope. They were just looking for a reason to fuck his high power talkin ass up. Lucky Tito nodded to them both, saying, "Alright Toker, alright homie, where's Ester at Capps?"

V-Capone pointed to the room and Tito strolled through Ester's door, holding his duffle bag and then throwing it on the bed when he walked in. Ester was asleep so Tito sat on the bed at her side, bouncing up and down, rubbing on her and saying, "Get up sleepy-head, that's all you do is sleep all day and party all night. Get your sexy ass up."

Ester whined under the covers, "Leave me alone Tito, I'm coming down. I'm burnt out."

Tito pulled the blankets off Ester and she was a sight for sore eyes. She was lying on her stomach, half naked, but had on a pink bra and matching G-string.

Lucky Tito said, "I told you don't fuck with that crystal, it's poison.

Shit'll fuck you all up." He spanked her ass.

Ester yelled, "Stop you ass bite!"

Lucky Tito smiled and bit Ester right on her butt cheeks hard.

Ester jumped and complained, "Ewe you motherfucker, that shit hurt, bastard."

Tito kissed Ester saying, "Now you can call me an ass bite and know it's true."

Ester lay on her back looking hella sexy. The front side of her panties had red writing, "2 NASTY 4 U." written on them. Lucky Tito licked his lips lustfully, admiring Ester's figure, her six pack and thick inner thighs, size C-cup tits and tight gap between her legs. Lucky Tito started kissing her belly button, going lower to her inner thighs and then rubbing on her snatch.

She moaned and said, "Stop Tito, I don't feel good babe."

Tito said, "I'll make you feel hella good right now, don't trip."

Ester was playing hard to get. She played the same song and dance every time Tito came over. Ester was Tito's sancha, his old standby. He'd come to her to get away from Tina when Tina would trip on him and it became too much for him to bear.

Ester lay with her eyes closed, then asked, "Aye do you got that twenty-dollars you owe me? I wanna buy a sack and get right."

Lucky Tito unzipped his duffle bag and pulled out a stack of hundreds, putting a hundred in her bra and two hundred in her panties.

He threw the rest of the stack on her belly, saying, "I don't got no change, but here's a few hundred for all the times I borrowed money."

Ester pulled the bill out of her bra and said, "Few hundred my ass, what are these, one-dollar bills..." She opened her eyes and looked at the one-hundred dollar bills in surprise. "What the fuck, how'd you get this paper?" she jumped up quickly and looked in the duffle bag.

Lucky Tito peeled off eight, one-hundred dollar bills and gave them to her saying, "Here's next month's rent. Stay outta my bag girl, I got bricks in there."

Ester saw the brick of heroin and pulled it out excitedly. "Damn, what the fuck! Who'd you rob?"

Lucky Tito put the brick back into the duffle bag and zipped it. He looked over his shoulder and noticed Jacker was standing there in the hallway checking them out so he asked, "What's cracking homie?"

Joker just nodded, "Nothing, just goin to the bathroom," he said strolling away.

Tito shut the bedroom door, unzipped his pants and told Ester, "I'm blessing you with the business, paper, and chunks so you best come correct with some skull and I'm talking about a blowjob that'll make me have a seizure!"

Ester was on the bed doggy-style sticking her tongue ring out looking like a nasty snake, flirting and teasing. She gave Tito head then sat next to him and asked, "Ok, so what's really going on? I can tell something's wrong."

Lucky Tito lay down and told Ester about everything that had happened. She sat there with her mouth open in disbelief. None of this was the Tito she knew. She realized the crooked cop had pushed him over the edge.

Lucky Tito lay on Ester saying, "I want you." He began pulling her panties off but she pushed his hand off saying, "Pendejo quit acting dumb. You need to control that heroin hard on and head to Mexico a.s.a.p.!"

Tito was loaded and spinning off the pills and the shot he'd done earlier and he just wanted to lay in bed with Ester and just fuck all night. He knew that wasn't the smart thing to do though so he got up and told her, "Fuck it, you want a shot? I'm going to fix one up... shit-I'll fix five, ten, fifteen up. I'm ballin and I got it like that now baby doll! Sex, drugs, money and gangsta rap, fuck rock n roll."

Ester saw she was going to have to help Tito because he was on some other old crazy shit and was losing sight of reality. She wiped the sand out of her eyes and put her hair in a ponytail, looking at herself in the mirror. Lucky Tito put a full syringe in his arm and squirted the whole shot in his vein. Ester grabbed the syringe from him when he was done, "Aye stupid why'd you do that much? You're going to overdose and die! If you OD then the ambulance and cops will show up and you're through. You'll be in prison for life. Kick back babe," she said.

Tito lay back in bed with his hands behind his head saying, "So what, I'm a dead man walking either way. This way I die falling out a cloud nine, babeee...."

Ester smacked him on his face and told him, "Shut up stupid. Don't act like that, you aint dyin. You're winning the game but you gotta get ghost to Mexico."

They started playfully wrestling then Lucky Tito said, "I can't drive. Come with me babe, I need your help. You'll come up big time with me. We'll be like Bonnie and Clyde."

Ester popped a few Oxycodone pills and shot up 30 mm of heroin, then said, "Fuck this shit's good, I feel like I'm gonna cum on myself." She stuck her fingers in her pussy and started bangin her g-spot. The dope's rush was intense, mixed with the sex she was about to have.

Lucky Tito said, "Looks like I'm getting lucky, ooweee!" He pulled her fingers out of her panties and sucked on them. She was already stripping naked. Tito opened her lips and licked and sucked on her clit. Ester was moaning and pumping into his face, holding the back of his head. Tito was high as fuck and he felt her cum so he got on top of her and slid in her saying, "Fuck you're tight as fuck! You got that bomb pussy."

He opened his eyes and saw his wife Tina's face. Ester was moaning and whining saying Tito's name, but Tito was hearing Tina moan and say his name. Dude was hallucinating on a good trip or maybe Tito's alter ego Lucky was fucking Ester and Tito was justifying his having sex with Ester in that sense. Either way, homie was out of his mind, but he knew his heart belonged to Tina.

Meanwhile, in the kitchen, V-Capone, Toker, Jacker and Angela were smoking meth, passing a pipe around. Jacker blew out a cloud of smoke and finally spoke on something he'd been thinking about for the last two hours. Jacker was actually plotting on Tito, but didn't know if he could pull the jack lick off because Toker and V-Capone weren't his homeboys and he didn't know how close they were to Lucky Tito. Plus, there was the no kicking up dust at his sister's house rule.

Jacker finally passed the pipe to V-Capone and asked, "Aye, how tight are you fools with that kat Tito in the room?"

V-Capone blew smoke toward Jacker playing mind games and being disrespectful. Then he said, "That's my boy. Why, what's crackin?"

Toker said, "Yeah Lucky's straight, that's the homie. He shot up some enemies with us before when we needed help. He's a rider, but he just likes getting high mostly, why you askin?"

Jacker put his hat on backwards, mad-dogged and mean-mugged the circle saying, "I wanna jack that fool. I saw a gang of dope and money in his duffle bag; I'm talking thousands and a couple of bricks dawg."

The circle laughed and Angela said, "You're hallucinating bro. Tito's broke. That fool's always borrowing five dollars, twenty dollars here and there. He's probably trying to borrow money from Ester right now."

V-Capone said, "Yeah Lucky aint in the game like that dawg. And if he was, you aint jackin him, that's my dawg like I said."

Jacker looked at V-Capone sideways. "Whatcha mean I aint jackin him if he was ballin! I jack fools all day every day, that's why I'm called Jacker! You ain't runnin my program fool. I jack who I want ese!" Jacker said.

Toker was blowing his crystal smoke into Angela's mouth, then French kissing her.

She said, "That's a real shot gun blast baby."

V-Capone got up in Jackers face and tension was in the air when V-Capone said, "Who the fuck you talkin to like that fool, I'll smash your ass if you come at me sideways like that again!"

Angela got in between them both and said, "Kick back aye, you're fuckin up my high, no fighting here. Kick back carnal! Don't be getting crazy with the homie or you can't post up here." Then she told Toker, "Grab V-Cappz babe, quit trippin you guys!"

Toker said, "Kick it dawg. You vatos are trippin over nada; Lucky aint got it like that aye."

Jacker said, "Man I know what I saw. If I'm trippin then let's go see what's in that duffle bag."

Jacker sat on the counter, Angela started washing dishes and V-Capone pulled two Budweiser's out of the fridge and handed one to Toker saying, "Naw man, what Lucky Tito gots in his bag is his business. Kill game, it aint happenin."

Toker said, "Aye Tito's got priors for robbin connections so he might've come up, but not like Jackers talkin bout. He'd break bread and get us high if he did. Don't trip he's cool like that, but all that pushin up on the homie tryin to pressure him and jackin aint gonna work. He aint no sucker, just kick it Jacker."

Jacker jumped off the counter trying to walk toward the room but V-Capone and Toker blocked him. Jacker said, "I work for the Mafia and Lucky aint my homie. He's gotta pay a tax to the brotherhood since he's in my Varrio and if you vatos got something to say about it, I'll just let the mob know you two stepped on their toes and wouldn't let me collect! I know you don't want a green light thrown on your asses. So either you're with me or against me. What is it?"

V-Capone and Toker looked at each other as if communicating by mental telepathy thinking, *this foo wants to die, let's kill him.*

Angela didn't even want to get involved with this one. Her brother was playing the mob card and he did have some juice and authority in the hood, given to him by the Mexican Mafia locked up in Pelican Bay. Jacker was their hands on the streets. He would jack and tax gangsters and send some of the money to the mobsters' books or money to take care of their families.

V-Capone and Toker both knew they were now walking a thin line and could easily get a contract put out on their lives. They were just simple gangbangers and the Mexican-Mob controlled the streets as well as the pen.

It wasn't always like that, but so many youngsters going to prison wanted power and money and were eager to make a name for themselves so the mob manipulated the young G's using them as foot soldiers, making them think they were moving up in the ranks. But the cold truth was that the mob was just using and abusing those soldiers because they came a dime a dozen and they knew that every one of them was disposable.

Angela knocked on Ester's door and Ester unlocked it saying, "What do you want bitch?" She went back and lay on the bed next to Tito as Angela walked in. Angela saw a gang of money and dope, but not the full brick and stash that Jacker had talked about so she said, "Ay my bro's trippin-he wants to jack you Tito."

Tito in a cold nod, eyes closed heard this and said, "Is that right? Tell em come get some if he wants some. I gotta hot nine with 17 shots for his bitchass!" Tito cocked back his pistol still lying in bed.

Angela said, "Oh hell no!" Then she walked out, closed the door and walked up to her brother and hugged him, whispering in Toker's ear, "Tito does have a gang of shit and money."

Angela pushed her brother Jacker toward the door to break up the macho standoff and despite what she had just told her brother secretly, she said aloud, "Just leave bro, Lucky don't got shit. I checked his bag."

He strolled away with his hand on his pistol saying, "You're lying bitch! This aint over V-Cappz, I'll see you on the streets, I got your ass ese!" He then pointed two fingers at the gangsters, shooting an imaginary gun.

V-Capone got pissed, pulled his real gun out and pointed it at Jacker, chasing him out of the pad.

Angela blocked V-Capone, who said, "I play with real guns puto. Puro Northside Redlands! Fuck Varrio Redlands, go hide behind the Mafia you crybaby. I don't give a fuck about none of that bullshit. This is Northside on mines!"

Angela slammed the door and then ran back into Ester's room.

Ester asked, "What the fuck's crackin out there bitch? Kill the racket!"

Toker looked out the blinds and saw Jacker heading up Sun Street, walking towards Tribune Street, probably heading to the OG Gino's pad to cross them up. V-Capone and Toker both knew Jacker was going to politic on them and their names would end up in the hat. Then half the hood would be trying to kill them to earn a name with the

Mafia and possibly even get made. Jacker was scandalous like that. He was going to go cry to the other veteranos working for the Mob and it would be all bad.

They both went into Esters room and Toker asked Tito, "Aye homie you came up huh?"

They wanted to test Lucky and see if he was worth getting into a jam over. People change when they come up on loot and act as if they don't know their homies sometimes.

V-Capone was looking in the bag, he asked, "Aye Lucks, how about looking out for me and Toker? We're on the run. Parole's looking for us. Help us get on our feet dawg."

Lucky Tito got up, scratching his nose he said, "Man dawg, I'm fucked up. I thought I was at home. How'd I end up in Redlands? What did you say Cappz?"

Toker said, "Will you help us out with some goods?"

Lucky Tito said, "Oh Yeah, fo sho that! This aint nada, let me break this brick up real quick, I got you both, Ester too. Here's a couple hundred." He handed them some money and V-Capone and Toker smiled, knowing they were right about backing up Lucky.

V-Capone said, "Gracias, I got something to do. I'll be back right now. Let's roll Tokes."

They both sprinted down the street in the cuts and background and alleys, trying to catch up to Jacker before he reached Gino's pad on Tribune Street. Gino ran the neighborhood for the Mob and once Jacker got in Gino's ear and told him what happened, V-Capone and Toker would be put on the hit list.

But only if Jacker made it.

They were hitting fences as if the police were chasing them. But they were the ones hunting this time. They saw Jacker walking down Sun Street and then making a left on Tribune. Toker pulled his bandana over his face and pulled his hat down low. V-Capone pulled his bandana up but he was bald, still, one-half of his head was hidden. He started running down the alley trying to cut off Jacker and made it just I time. Now Jacker was walking toward him. V-Capone was snaking through the cars on the street. Toker was using the same exact tactics, creeping from behind quickly but carefully.

Gino's house was five or six houses behind V-Capone. He saw gangsters in the front yard drinking, bumping music and washing a Low Rider. There were maybe seven G's banged out, posted up.

V-Capone knew if Jacker got any closer to Gino's pad, most likely there'd be a shootout and he was trying to put this hit down quick-like a hit and run type of shit.

Just then, Jacker crossed the street and Toker ran up behind him. Pop! Pop! Pop! The Colt 380 bucked into Jackers back. He turned and the adrenaline made him run as his instincts kicked in. V-Capone ran up from the front. Pop! Pop! Pop! Pop! Pop! He let off the 25, all in Jackers chest and legs.

There was a giant monster style truck nearby and Jacker crawled up under the truck for safety. V-Capone and Toker ran up to the truck and emptied their clips off under the truck. Jacker was screaming for his life like a ho.

V-Capone heard voices from up the street yelling at him and Toker. "What's crackin ese?" The G's at Gino's flashed their pistols.

V-Capone and Toker were out of bullets so they cut out and started hitting fences, hoping the bullets they put into Jacker were enough to murder his punk ass.

Up the block, hiding behind a building in an alley they took their bandanas off their faces and took off the clothes they were wearing and threw their clothes away in a dumpster, so that they'd look different than the suspects. Most gangsters on missions wore baggy clothes because they had a set of shorts or other clothes underneath for this exact purpose. It also made it easy to conceal assault rifles and hand guns. They were both now wearing shorts and tank tops which was opposite of the Ben Davis uniforms they'd been wearing. They walked out of the alley and blended into the neighborhood acting as normal as they could.

There was an old man watering his grass and some kids were playing kickball in the street. Toker kicked the ball when it went his way. They both looked like two regular dudes just walking down the street in broad daylight.

V-Capone looked at his watch. It was 4:45. "It'll be dark in fifteen minutes. Let's split up and meet at Ester's." he said.

Gino's pack of gangsters were in his front yard pissed off. Gino was at Jackers side as he was lifted into the ambulance. He was hit, but still alive. Earlier Gino had asked Jacker who'd shot him, but he was out of it so he never got an answer.

The cop pushed Gino aside and asked Jacker, "Who shot you sir? Were they gang members?" The cop looked toward Gino's house suspiciously.

Gino knew his house would probably get hit by a police raid, so he interrupted the cop saying, "My homeboy don't know who shot him, leave him alone!"

Gino planned on holding street court, smoking whoever had shot Jacker. But Jacker needed to tell them who did it. Right now wasn't the time so he'd go visit him at the hospital later and get the info.

The cop pushed Gino ordering him away, "Get out of here!"

Gino moved away to the side of the ambulance and out of Jackers sight, but still listening as he was concerned about his homeboy.

The cop asked Jacker, "Son who shot you?"

Jacker lifted his head and didn't see Gino so he said, "V-Capone and Toker, Northside Redlands shot me. They're at a house on the corner of Sun and Alta at my sister's pad. They got a lot of dope in that house too. Fuck them fools!"

Jacker put his head down and the cops shut the doors. They saw Gino standing right there and gave him a dirty look.

Gino walked up to his house full of homies. He was shocked and disgusted at what he had just heard.

Gino and Jackers homeboys were eager to retaliate and started asking Gino questions. "Who shot Jacker, are we goin on a mission tonight? Who we killin dog?" They asked.

Gino sat on his porch and put his feet up relaxing, drinking a 40 oz. of 211. All he said was, "Jackers a rat. He snitched to the cops that V-Capone and Toker from Northside shot him. Jackers no good. He's green lighted. Don't trip on Toker or V-Capone, as far as I'm concerned, only thing wrong they did was to let Jacker live. We'll finish him off when he gets out of the hospital. We're cleaning house. Fuck a snitch! We'll play like all good with Jacker, make him feel comfortable. We'll get high, then take him to the orange groves, throw gasoline on him and light his ass on fire. We'll make sure he dies with the Varrios secrets. It's mandatory, Jackers getting rubbed out!"

All of Jackers homeboys couldn't believe what Gino said. They were all disappointed and distraught, as if the Jacker they knew had already died.

Jackers dawg, Richie Rich said, "I wish Jacker would've died and went out like a hood legend, instead of living and going out like a rat. It's all bad!"

All the love and respect for Jacker instantly turned into hate, and just like that, one of the hood's top soldiers lost rank and became number one on the Varrio hit list! That's how the game goes when gangstas play hardball. V-Capone and Toker had actually accomplished their mission when all was said and done, even if Jacker lived. Jacker lost all street credibility, so no matter what he told Gino about them, the info would be disregarded.

Stupid Jacker struck out in the game, livin that thug life. Yoouu'rree outta here!

Angela popped some pills and did a shot of heroin. She was up on crystal and down on heroin, feeling like she was on a roller coaster. The radio was bumping, Dub 'C', "Get This Party Started Now," and Angela was dancing hella gangster freaky in slow motion, throwing gang signs and stripping her clothes off down to her panties. She repeated Dub 'C's' lyrics,[iv]

"Let's get this party started now,
Can't stop, won't stop til the one time break us
Claimin we disturbin the neighbors,
Cuz it's on at the home girl's house
("Plus I got the bomb ass head that'll set Tito free, a ghetto bitch down to fuck")

Angela changed the lyrics a bit, flirting with Lucky Tito.

Lucky laughed and said, "Hell Yeah that's what I'm talkin about. Take it all off girl! It's hot in here."

Angela shook her ass at Tito so he reached out to spank her, but instead he caught a left slap across his face from Ester.

She said, "Aye stupid don't even think about it. She's my doggy and you're *my* one and only Lucky baby." She kissed him, straddling him and telling Angela, "Put your clothes on bitch."

Angela flipped her off and kept dancing, enjoying her high saying, "All of a sudden some bitch is a hater instead of a player, miss me with that drag."

Lucky Tito pushed Ester off him and went to shoot up another fix. He told Ester, "Keep it 100 playgirl. All that I'm your one and only game ain't flyin. You're my sancha, that's it. We fuck, we get high and that's it, that's all. Angela's your doggy right? I share everything with my dawgs, cash, dope and pussy, so what now?"

Ester's feelings got hurt, but she knew Tito was telling the truth. Those hurt feelings could easily be mended with a shot of good feelings and a few more pills though, so Ester said, "Alright, ya you're right, whatever. I share all my men with this bitch anyways, you ain't special."

She tried to make Tito jealous and he knew it. He hugged her from behind as she slammed a fix and kissed her neck.

"Ewe I'm jealous girl, cut it out already," he joked with her. He bit her neck saying, "You're all talk Ester. Your panties read '2 nasty 4 u', but you ain't actin like it. I'm the one that's too nasty for *you*. Time to show and prove, let's groove."

Angela was still dancing and throwing up gang signs at Tito and Ester. Angela stuck her tongue out at Ester and said, "Bitch get off that hater shit. You weren't yelling and moaning Lucky's name two nights ago when Bugsy was fucking your brains out, so move around with that one and only bullshit."

Ester said, "Oh now you're tellin on the homegirl huh bitch? Fuck it."

Lucky laughed saying, "Ewe, busted!"

Ester said, "Do what you want Lucky! Just don't fall in love Angela and don't let Toker find out."

Lucky stood up and asked, "You're Toker's girl Angela?"

Angela strolled up to Tito's face and kissed him saying, "Not even that, he's just a fuck like you're just a fuck. She unzipped his pants and got on her knees."

Lucky said, "I'm gonna have to tell Toker not to kiss you today. Ha-ha crazy hood-rat."

Ester laughed and tried to kiss Tito saying, "How do you know if I didn't suck a dick today?"

Tito pushed her mouth away saying, "You're right cochina, now get to double teaming my cock with your doggy dog!" Then Ester and Angela both gave Lucky head.

Ester said, "Keep sucking after he cums and he'll squirm and shake like he's having a seizure."

Angela just laughed and said, "No problem."

Tito was lying on the bed with two of Redland's finest freaks and felt like he was in heaven.

Yet, he was distracted by the devils that were hot on his trail. He was on a path of destruction and death was right around the corner, floating his way.

9TH INNING STRETCH
PRESENT DAY, MAY 5TH 2008-5:30 P.M.

Redlands PD Gang Task Force was suited and booted, preparing for a gang sweep raid. V-Capone and Toker were their targets. An unmarked cop car cruised slowly by Ester and Angela's house, the Northside hangout. Officer Sanchez noticed an older gang member strolling out of the house and opening the passenger door of a white Avalanche truck, digging around inside it, searching for something. Officer Sanchez kept driving but jotted down the license plate number. His computer showed that the vehicle was stolen and that the suspect was wanted for murdering a Colton cop and a Mafia member and a string of robberies. Bold letters on his computer screen warned ARMED AND DANGEROUS. Officer Sanchez thought, *Jackpot! But this could get ugly. What kind of gangster is killing mafia members and cops? He must have a death wish.*

A Redlands PD lieutenant got ahold of Colton PD's Sgt. Garza and let him know the gang task force was about to raid a spot and there was a possibility that Tito Lucky Lopez was in the house. He knew there were active warrants for him and he gave Sgt. Garza the courtesy and respect of joining the raid, since Officer Yang, the murdered officer had been one of Sgt. Garza's men. Sgt. Garza got on his radio and announced Tito Lopez's whereabouts and a fleet of cop cars in Colton headed to Redlands. Officer Alex Lara was in San Bernardino cruising around off radar, still hunting for Tito, when his radio crackled and he got the good news. He threw a U-turn and drove at speeds of 120 mph to Redlands on a long back street.

There was a Stater Bros. Supermarket across the street from Ester and Angela's pad. Their view of it was the back of the store. What they didn't know was that the Gang Task Force was gathered in the store's parking lot on the front side. There were two snipers on the roof looking down at Ester's pad with scopes aimed at the windows. They couldn't see anything inside because the blinds were closed. It was already dark too, so the snipers couldn't be seen either. They held their post until Colton PD arrived. When they did, they'd move on the raid together. There was no sign of V-Capone or Toker yet. One sniper noticed a Colton squad car pull into the Thrifty Gas station at the corner of Sun and Orange Streets. A cop got out and the sniper got on his radio, "Sir, there's movement at the gas station. A Colton officer just pulled up. He must not have gotten the memo to meet in front of Stater Bros., and if the suspects spot him, he might spook them and fuck up the raid. Somebody radio him and tell him to get out of there!"

A voice on the other side of the radio responded, "Hold him down. Roger that."

Officer Alex Lara blended in with the shadows as he jumped over the short grey brick wall into the alley. He looked left, looked right, and then jumped over a wired fence. He startled a family of people watching TV in their living room and put his finger to his mouth, warning them, "Shhh," and he kept on creeping. He spotted the stolen white Avalanche truck and knelt down next to it, pulled out a knife and slashed all four tires. *He aint drivin outta here,* he thought. Lara then crept up to a window, but he couldn't see inside because the blinds were closed. He inched his way over to the door and turned the doorknob but the door was locked. He heard voices and music playing inside and decided to creep around to the back yard and see if he could find a way in. He saw a light flashing off and on, on the house walls, but he just disregarded it and crept to the backyard.

The snipers were on the radio having a fit. "Boss we got some CPD hot dog moving on the house by himself. We flash lighted him but he ignored the signal. Is this the respect we're being shown by CPD?"

Hearing this, the lieutenant ordered, "Fucking ass holes! All cars move in slowly, move in!"

Lucky Tito felt like a gangsta playa macadocious looking at Ester eat out Angela's pussy. Both freaks were moaning, going at it like nymphomaniacs. Tito was drained. He'd gotten his issue of pussy and was smoking a cigarette, chewing some pills and enjoying the show.

He said, "Damn Ester, you eat pussy better than I do, you nasty ho. Ha-ha." He spanked her ass as she started finger-banging Angela.

She said, "A girl knows what a girl likes. Go to the gas station store for some wine coolers and some cigarettes Yeah?"

Tito said, "Yeah I'm on it." He put his pants on and slipped on a slingshot. He picked up his 9 mm gloc and stared down the barrel of the gun for a few seconds, remembering where he'd gotten it and why he was being hunted before putting it in his pocket. He tensed up and his smile left his face as reality kicked in. He was hella dizzy and groggy. His body was telling him that he'd already done too much heroin and pills today. Tito was going to see if the freaks could trade some heroin for crystal so he could wake up out of his stupor and get back on the agenda. He pocketed a couple hundred and strolled into the living room. It was dark and he tripped over the laundry basket and fell to the floor.

"What the fuck ay!" he complained. Then Tito heard two gunshots zoom over his head, Pop! Pop!

"You're going to die Lucky," he heard someone yell at him. Pop! Pop! Two more shots ripped through the door. Lucky Tito looked to his right and saw Alex Lara standing by the sliding glass door shooting at him. Tito got lucky again, dodging all four bullets. He crawled behind the wall in the hall and shot back at Alex. Pop! Pop! Pop! Pop!

He yelled, "You're gonna die Alex! Fuck your life bitch!"

Shots ricocheted through the kitchen. Alex Lara yelled in pain as a hot bullet bit at his ear. Blood leaked onto his uniform as he ducked for cover. His rage and hate pushed him forward as he moved to the other side of the sliding door, so that he'd have a better chance of shooting Tito. All Alex saw was red as he charged in like a bull, but Lucky Tito wasn't having it. He jumped up and blasted at Lara, Pop! Pop! Pop! Then he ducked out again. All of the bullets hit Officer Lara in the chest and he flew back into the backyard and rolled for cover. Only his bulletproof vest had saved his ass.

Lucky Tito yelled, "Your bitch ass won't try that again huh puto!" Lucky laughed and aimed at the window. All was quiet and Ester and Angela came running out of the bedroom.

Angela yelled, "What the fuck, aye don't be playing with your gun in my pad aye!"

Lucky Tito yelled, "Get back in the room!" But it was too late.

Officer Lara blasted twice, Pop! Pop!-hitting Angela in the shoulder. She screamed and fell back into Ester's arms, who then pulled her back toward the room.

Tito jumped in their direction, still shooting at Alex Lara. Pop! Pop! Lara shot back in rapid succession. Pop! Pop! Pop! Pop! Pop! Tito fell in the hall. He'd been shot in the ankle.

Lara re-loaded his weapon and then used his baton to knock out all the rooms' windows trying to get a better view of Lucky's location. The blinds were still up though so he couldn't see clearly.

Ester ran to the restroom and wet a towel, then ran back and put pressure on Angela's wounds with the towel. She had been shot in the shoulder and stomach.

Tito yelled, "Fuck aye, keep pressure on her stomach! Don't let her bleed out aye. Fuck, she needs a doctor ASAP!" He hopped down the hall to sneak a peek at Lara but didn't see nothing.

All was quiet except for the sound of Angela crying loudly.

"It hurts mija! Help me! Call the ambulance, it hurts, I'm gonna die. Please don't let me die Lucky," she cried.

Alex Lara laughed wickedly saying, "Looks like I got your hood-rat homeboy! You're next Tito. You're a dead man walking!"

Tito crept to the other room and put his hand out the window, shooting in Alex Lara's direction.

"And you're just dead you punk bitch," Tito yelled. Pop! Pop! Pop! Pop! Pop!

Lara was caught off guard and was hit in his ass and right arm. He jumped up and sprinted around the side of the house intending to try to attack from the front side. He was surprised to see ten cop cars parked in front of the house in a semicircle with blue and red lights flashing. Their pistols were pointing at the house as they stood safely behind their squad cars. Officer Lara was tempted to start shooting at the officers, but he realized they didn't know he was crooked and they were there to back him up.

Lucky Tito hopped back to the restroom and washed his ankle, then tied it off with his grey bandana to stop the bleeding. "Do you got any 9 bullets or other guns, I'm outta ammo," he asked Ester. Ester was still helping Angela who was crying.

"Look in the attic, my brother has a 12 gauge with a gang of shells in the closet," she said.

Lucky Tito knew he couldn't jump up into the attic, so he called Ester over, "Come over here Ester, grab my duffle bag and pull out a chunk of dope."

Angela yelled, "No, no! Don't leave me mija please!"

Ester said, "Just for a second." She ran and swooped up the duffle bag and then Lucky Tito lifted Ester up to the attic.

He told Ester to stash the money and dope and get the gauge so she did just that and handed the gun down to Tito who kissed the 12 gauge

Mossberg and loaded it up saying, "This is my lifesaver. I can mow pigs down easier now. Hell Yeah! Fuck them fools!"

He looked out the window and saw Alex Lara and a grip of cop cars surrounding the pad and thought, *Oh shit, it's all bad! There are pigs everywhere out there.*

Redlands PD Sgt. Travis asked Officer Lara, "What's your problem son? Showboating and high signing? There are three armed killers in that house and you can't go in there like you're Doc Holiday. There's a cop killer in there as well."

Officer Lara was behind the cop car, ducking and holding his wounds and answered, "The cop killer is Tito Lopez. He killed my partner this morning. I don't think there are any other shooters inside the house, just two females."

Sgt. Travis understood Lara's anxious drive to arrest Tito so he stopped scolding him. By this time, the scene was like a circus sideshow. Fire truck and ambulance sirens screamed in the distance, heading to the Thrifty Gas Station. Police cars surrounded the whole block and the ghetto bird helicopter circled above, shining a bright light down over the house and yard. As the Colton PD started arriving, Officer Lara was escorted to the gas station where the paramedics started stripping off his uniform and examining his gunshot wounds.

All the while, his eyes stayed on the house. From where he was, he had a clear view of both the front and back yards and could see if anyone would try to leave either way.

In the house Tito was helping Ester take care of Angela.

Tito said, "Should we give her a shot of dope? It'll kill the pain."

Angela screamed, "Yeah the pain's killing me, give me a shot!"

He did a shot to calm down and he split the other one between Angela and Ester. Then he shoved a handful of oxycodone's in her mouth saying, "Here, this should help, just be quiet. I gotta think."

Ester was in the hallway hugging her best friend, who was under a blanket.

"It'll be okay. Just hold on mija, you'll be all right. Pray to God, he'll help us."

She rocked back and forth trying to console her best friend. Angela was relaxed, but getting weaker. She mumbled, "I don't wanna die mija, I feel like I'm dying."

Tito lightly slapped Angela's cheeks and telling her, "Wake up, you're not gonna die, don't crash girl."

Angela could only mumble a reply, "I'm tired and cold, help me."

Tito grabbed Angela and dragged her to the bathtub.

"Put the hot water on to warm her up," he ordered Ester. Then he asked, "Do you got any crystal? I think the heroin is putting her out and we need to keep her awake. Go fix up a shot of crystal for her, hurry!"

Ester ran to the room while Tito babysat Angela.

"You'll be alright. The ambulance is at the corner. I just gotta get you out there without getting us all smoked. These pigs aint playin fair," he told her.

Ester ran back in with the shot of crystal then squatted down and held onto Angela's arm tightly as Tito looked for a vein.

"She needs a hospital Tito. Let's just surrender so she can get help. There's nowhere to run, we're surrounded." Ester begged.

Tito found a vein and shot the meth up in Angela, who coughed because the potency and rush hit her. After it took effect, Angela was alert again, heart pumping fast, but better than not pumping at all. She had to pick her poison. She had to either be on a downer and be half-dead, feeling no pain, or be on an upper and alive feeling all the pain. By then Angela was in shock as she lay in a bathtub full of bloody water looking at her wounds.

"What happened Ester am I shot?" she asked as she tried to climb out of the tub. Ester knew her homegirl was way out of her mind. Tito let out the water and pushed her back down, handing Ester another towel to apply pressure to the wounds.

"Lay down Angela. The cops shot you. They're trying to kill us. Stay down, I'm holding down the fort," Tito told her.

Lucky Tito knew the gig was up and that they were in a no-win situation. He went and slammed some meth to get back to alert status. He didn't trust not one cop outside. Every single one of them would try to kill him as soon as he stepped outside.

He was awake now, but the heroin had him in a dream-like state of mind, a bad dream at that. He had to get Angela help. He wasn't going to let her die over his beef with the cops. Just then, he had a thought and he reached into his pocket and pulled out Ms. Ramirez of Internal Affairs' phone number. He grabbed Ester's cell phone and dialed the number. Tito Lopez got lucky once again, because Ms. Ramirez answered the call and he talked to her, telling her about the situation he was in.

He gave her directions to where he was at and said, "I'll turn myself into you, and only you. But you need to help my homegirl. Please get here ASAP! She's dying!"

Sgt. Travis was debriefing Sgt. Garza of the Colton PD on what had happened so far. Officer Lara was sitting in the ambulance all patched up. His wounds weren't that serious, but he was beating himself up because Tito had drawn blood first. Lara was watching the house for any movement. He had to be the one to escort Tito Lopez to the Police station! Lara decided to play the sympathy card with his boss so he went and spoke to both Sgt. Travis and Sgt. Garza.

"Boss you know that piece of shit killed my partner! You got to let me slap the cuffs on him sir."

Sgt. Garza yelled at Lara, "I don't got to do nothing! I ordered you to stand down and do the paperwork. Now you're over here shot and who knows who you shot in the house. Get back to your vehicle and don't move a muscle!" he ordered.

Sgt. Travis was surprised at the tongue-lashing Sgt. Garza gave his officer. He guessed something else was going on. Alex Lara just stood there, blood boiling, feeling disrespected.

Sgt. Garza yelled, "Get out of my face! You're dismissed!"

Lara stomped away; feeling pissed off and went to sit in his squad car. He left the door open, so he had a clear view of the front door of the house. Lara was plotting his next move.

Sgt. Garza told Sgt. Travis, "I've got an idea, I'll call Tito's mother and see if she can talk him out peacefully."

He pulled out his cell phone and dialed Victory Outreach's phone number. He identified himself and requested to speak with Denise Lopez after informing the pastor of the ongoing drama that was unfolding. Pastor Thomas put Denise on the phone.

"Hello?" Sgt. Garza said, "Hello Ms. Lopez I need you…"

Denise Lopez interrupted Sgt. Garza, "I don't care what you need, I don't know where Tito's at," she said as she tried to hang up the phone.

Pastor Thomas stopped her and said, "Denise, listen to him! Tito's surrounded and in trouble. He might be shot, and he already shot Alex Lara. Listen!"

Hearing this, Denise put the phone back up to her ear and asked, "What is it you want Officer Garza?"

Sgt. Garza saw the news media van drive up and rolled his eyes thinking, *great, just what we need.* He answered, "I want you to talk Tito into surrendering and coming out peacefully. The situation is already ugly. There are snipers ready to kill him if he makes any hostile moves and we don't want that. He loves you and will listen to you. We don't want him to die."

Denise Lopez yelled into the phone, "Damn liar! You're going to kill him slowly and put him on death row. Give me one reason I should help you!"

Sgt. Garza responded, "I'll give you two reasons. I know Tito didn't kill Yang, but he did commit many other crimes. That's one reason. Reason two is his son Frankie needs a father, even if he is locked up!"

His words convinced Denise, so she quickly got Tina and Frankie-Boy into the car and headed to Redlands to try to help save Tito's life. They prayed the whole way, but they knew they were dancing with devils in cop uniforms.

Something flew through the bedroom window and glass shattered everywhere. Tito expecting to feel and hear shock grenades go off, shot back at the window, BOOOM! Then he pointed the shotgun down the hallway. He was crouching in the restroom doorway and the girls were tucked away behind him. No pigs ran up, but he heard a phone ringing and thought, *Oh that's what it was.*

He quickly ducked down and picked up the phone and said, "What's crackin, who's this?"

The voice on the other end said, "Hey buddy my name is Charles. I'm a hostage negotiator. How many people are in there with you Chico?"

Tito yelled in the phone, "I don't got any hostages! My homegirl is shot asshole and my name ain't Chico stupid, it's Tito!"

Charles the negotiator quickly responded, "Calm down, Tito, my mistake. How can we resolve this peacefully? We don't want anybody else getting hurt!"

The crystal meth had Tito twisted and he began rambling on the phone. He yelled, "Alex shot him! Alex shot Yang, not me! He's tryin to set me up! Angela needs help, she's dying!"

He looked over at Angela who was slumped over unconscious. Ester was scared and yelled, "Tito she's knocked out. We need help! Tell them to let me bring her out, but not to shoot us!"

Tito told Charles just that and said, "I didn't kill no cops man serio, it's a setup. I'm gonna bring Angela and Ester to the door and let them go then as soon as Ms. Ramirez rolls up, I'll turn myself in peacefully."

Charles responded, "All of you can come out with your hands up. Take your shirts off so we can see that you aren't carrying weapons…"

Tito cut him off, "Naw, fuck that Chuck! Just Angela and Ester are coming out so don't shoot. When Ramirez shows up, I'll come out. I aint getting executed by them pigs, fuck that!"

Tito was looking out the window now and he waved at Charles and said, "I see you Chuck."

"I see you too Tito, who's Ramirez?" Charles said, "Let's not give these officers a reason to shoot you. Keep your weapon away from the door."

Tito laughed saying, "Oh Yeah, you're a funny guy. You got jokes sunshine," and he hung up the phone.

He called Ester to the bedroom as he cut a fat chunk of heroin, maybe 25 grams, wrapped it up in plastic and handed it to Ester. He got a syringe and broke it in half, then wrapped that up too and gave it to Ester saying, "Stick this stash in your pussy. When you go to court, I'll be on the county bus with you. Bring half the dope and syringe and hand it off to me on the bus. Get your half, get high and get you some store. I'll have my mom come pick up the bag in the attic and bail you out after court alright?"

Ester nodded in agreement, squatted down and stashed the dope and paraphernalia in her pussy. She knew the game; she'd been to jail before.

Tito was next. He got a ball of heroin, about an ounce, wrapped it up and squirted baby oil on it, then sat on the toilet and Tito stuck the ounce of heroin in his asshole.

Ester ignored him as he handled his business and picked up Angela, put her arm over her shoulder and whined, "Hurry up and help me Tito!"

Tito washed his hands saying, "Chasing that dragon in jail is too expensive for my blood. Come on, we'll get her out. Angela, wake up mija, you're getting help."

Tito wrapped a blanket around Angela and they carried her to the front door. His ankle was throbbing in pain, something sick now, and he felt a fever coming on. His whole foot was leaking blood but he hadn't realized it until now. Tito looked out of the window and saw the bright lights of the TV news people. He held the 12 gauge in one hand while Angela's arm was over his other shoulder and Ester held her up on the other side.

Tito opened the door saying, "Here goes its do or die Angela, literally! You'll be okay mija." He kissed her forehead and said, "God bless you!"

They were just about to walk out, and then Tito said, "Wait, who's that!"

HEY BATTER BATTER-SWING!
STRIKE 2, BALL 3
PRESENT DAY, MAY 5TH, 2008-9:25 P.M.

News reporter Olga Olspina was a gorgeous woman. She had long dark brown hair that flowed down to her ass. Her figure was voluptuous. Her curves were in all the right places. When she reported on a story for Fox 11 News, all eyes were on her. She was mesmerizing! She was standing at the Thrifty Gas Station holding a microphone, staring at Angela and Ester's house.

Her cameraman signaled her saying, "5, 4, 3, 2, 1..., we're live."

Olga Olspina took her cue and faced the camera saying, "This is Olga Olspina with Fox 11 News. We are reporting live from Redlands where there seems to be a standoff of some sort developing. Details are sketchy but from what I've overheard detectives discussing, there's a suspect barricaded in a house at the intersection of Sun and Alta Streets who apparently allegedly murdered a Colton officer early this morning. He also allegedly shot another officer in the City of Redlands and is suspected of committing a string of other crimes during a vicious crime spree earlier today."

Olga instructed the cameraman to point his camera up towards the Stater Bros Market's roof.

Then she said, "This is a dead serious situation. There are snipers on the rooftops, a SWAT team on location, and I believe there is a hostage negotiator who has made contact and is speaking to the suspect now. I have no information as of yet as to who the suspect is."

The cameraman panned the camera to the front door of the house and zoomed in as she reported.

Olga got into position and exclaimed, "It looks like the front door is opening! The suspect may be surrendering as we speak. Officers are maneuvering around their vehicles. Some are walking to the grassy area with bulletproof shields up and ready. They may be looking for a clear shot in case the suspect comes out shooting or acting aggressively! Who knows what they're thinking at this point. Paramedics are standing close by as well. It's possible that the suspect or his hostages may be hurt!"

Olga excitedly walked closer to the scene. That red skirt suit she was wearing made her stand out in the crowd, turning heads. Even the cameraman lost focus on the house as he followed Olga. The camera was focused on Olga's upside down heart-shaped thick ass. That should get a few more viewers!

Sgt. Garza and Sgt. Travis got the signal to 'come over' from hostage negotiator Charles. Right then for the second time, Officer Lara played the sympathy card with Sgt. Garza.

He walked over holding his wounds saying, "Sarge I need to talk to you."

Sgt. Garza said, "Not right now Lara. Tito's surrendering."

He walked away but Lara followed Garza saying, "Sarge I want to escort that piece of shit to the station. He took out my partner sir!" Lara played the humble role this time and brought out the water works. Fake tears trickled down his face, probably motivated by him imagining himself on Death Row. "Yang's dead because of that menace!" he cried.

Sgt. Garza looked back at Lara, then walked up to his face and stared dead into his eyes as if trying to read Lara's thoughts. He stared him down as if he was stealing Lara's darkest secrets and crimes, invading his lost soul through the windows of his tainted eyes. Lara broke eye contact, looking down at his shoes, wiping the fake tears away. Sgt. Garza said, "Hhhmmm," and then smiled, tapping Lara's shoulders as if comforting him. "Lara I know you're hurting and I know what happened. I know what Tito did and did not do. It's affected three police departments. So gain your composure son. A lot of people are going to have questions for you son and you'd better have the right answers. You represent this department. Let me get Tito into custody and then I'll see about letting you escort him to the county jail. Stay strong Lara, this is almost over!"

Lara had mixed emotions. Did his Sarge know what he'd done? But if he did then why did he say he'd allow Lara to escort Tito to the county? Lara was baffled because he knew that the Sarge didn't give anything up. Everything could mean either or. Sgt. Garza smiled and walked away to post up by Sgt. Travis and the negotiator Charles.

Tension was thick and all officers were on edge, trigger fingers itching, they were just looking for an excuse to snuff Tito Lopez and anyone with him out! A couple of fellow officers' blood had been shed that day and these blood sucking vampire cops were anxious to draw blood back. *Eye for an eye, life for a life. Shoot first, ask questions later*, was the motto of the day. No rights would be read to this criminal! Tito…you have the right to remain silent-nope! The way these pigs felt, they didn't think Tito had the right to breathe!

Officer Lara was standing behind his cruiser door, parked along the side of the house, holding a M-16 assault rifle, pointing it at the front door of the house. He planned to blindside Tito when he came out with a kill shot to his temple. The scope and infrared beam was on and the rifle was working perfectly. Finger on the trigger, Lara knew that his own life was at stake as well.

Lara was confident that his bosses and the courts would believe his story over that of a dope fiend like Tito Lopez, no problem. But Internal Affairs would be gunning for him, trying to twist him up in another long investigation. He already imagined that he would be suspended on paid leave or maybe with no pay at all. He couldn't afford that. A lot was on the line and when Tito stepped into the line of fire the red dot would land on his temple then one squeeze and poof! He'd lay dead in his tracks. That's it, that's all. He'd probably have a gun nearby. It would be justified homicide and then all the boys in blue would deem Officer Alex Lara a hero. No one would blame him.

A car came screeching to a halt behind him. This got Lara's attention. He could not believe his eyes. Tito's mom and two men, pastors, he guessed, had gotten out of a blue Cadillac and was apparently trying to talk someone out of the backseat of the car. The person finally stepped out, wiping tears from her sad eyes. It was Alex Lara's first and only love, Tito's wife, Tina Espinoza Lopez. Lara tightened his jaw, somewhat mesmerized with Tina's beauty. His heart was pounding and yearning for her love and embrace. He felt warm and aroused.

Tina stood scanning the sea of blue cop uniforms. She felt someone staring at her. She turned and saw Alex Lara holding an M-16, mouth open in awe, staring and smiling at her. He felt like giving her a comforting hug, so he began walking towards her.

Suddenly she began screaming at him. She was pointing at him with pure hate in her face, eyes and heart as she stomped his way. Her growls pierced his heart when she yelled, "I fuckin hate your ass you son of a bitch. I hate your guts you pussy coward, you aint about nada you pig bitch!"

Both pastors grabbed Tina, holding her back and telling her, "Relax Tina, he's not worth it. God will deal with him. Just relax, calm down."

Tina turned back toward Lara, yelling at the pastors, "It's his fault! HE killed the cop, not Tito. He's setting my HUSBAND up!" She put emphasis on the words 'my husband' in order to pierce Alex's heart and soul. She knew Alex still loved her and always would.

Hearing the commotion, Olga Olspina and her cameraman came running toward Tina and the pastors, who had put Tina in the car.

Olga asked, "Excuse me Miss, did you say something about a setup? Would you care to elaborate, who set whom up?"

Olga shoved the microphone in Tina's direction but Pastor Rick pushed the microphone away saying, "Please go away; my sister is having a hard time right now."

Pastor Thomas sat in the back seat, hugging Tina who was sobbing uncontrollably by then.

Denise Lopez quickly spotted Sgt. Garza and strolled over to his side. They exchanged words and Sgt. Garza handed Denise a cellphone.

Corrupted Officer Lara gripped his M-16 again and refocused his vision on the house's door. He mumbled, "Oh you hate me huh Tina? I'll give you a real reason to hate me dumb bitch. You want to play with hearts; I'll play with hearts then!" He looked through the scope saying, "fuck you bitch! You're a hoe anyways."

He knew damn well that she wasn't a hoe and had only been with him and Tito, but just seeing her fucked his whole mind up. He tried to lie to himself though and was having a hard time convincing himself. She had him twisted.

Lucky Tito was hella loaded, spinning, standing at the window looking for Alex Lara's bitch ass. When he scanned the crowd outside all he saw was a battalion of coppers with hate on their faces. He nervously laughed and cracked a fake smile. He was about to close the blinds when he did a double take. He swore he saw his mother standing out there with a phone to her ear. Just then, his phone rang and he grabbed up saying, "Moms, is that you!"

Denise waved and calmly answered, "Yes mijo. Sgt. Garza called me down here. He wants you to come out peacefully. He says that he'll guarantee your safety Tito."

Sgt. Garza was nodding, 'yes' and whispering something in his mother's ear.

Denise repeated it to her son. "He says to unload your guns and throw them outside the door. Strip down to your boxers and then help the hurt girl out. Lay her on the grass and then you lay on the grass on your stomach spread eagle."

Lucky Tito ached because even though his mom was trying to act calm, he saw right through all that. He felt her fear and pain within her cracking voice. Tito asked, "Can I trust him moms? Can I, should I?"

"Yes mijo, I think you can." Denise answered.

Tito saw a white Crown Victoria pull up behind where his mother and Garza were standing. Tito felt some hope when he saw Ms. Ramirez of Internal Affairs get out of the car. She was putting a bulletproof vest on as she started walking toward Sgt. Travis and Sgt. Garza. When he saw that they were talking to her, briefing her on the situation he felt somewhat safe. He told his mother, "Okay I'll surrender, just give me five minutes. Tell Ms. Ramirez to call me back in five. I love you mom."

Tito threw the gloc out the front door. Officer Yang's gloc. Then he shut the door without locking it. He put the 12 Mossberg pump next to the front door so he'd have easy access to it. Then he told Ester to give him the house key. He checked the backyard for cops and not seeing any, stepped out a few steps, just enough to reach over to the fuse box and threw the house key in it. He'd put it there so that later on his mom could get in the house and get the duffle bag. That way she would be able to bail Ester out and have the money and dope. He wasn't sure if she'd do that and for sure she would probably flush the dope but he had bigger things to worry about.

Angela and Ester were already stripped down to their bra and panties from the freak session. Tito unzipped his Frisco Ben pants and stripped down to his boxers. He was chewing on a whole handful of some tramadol, Oxycotins and morphine pills and swallowing them down with a beer.

The phone rang and Tito grabbed it and said, "Hello," as he looked out through the blinds and saw that Ms. Ramirez was on the phone. She was standing next to his mother and Sgt. Garza.

The voice on the other end answered, "Hello Tito. It's Ms. Ramirez. Are you ready to come out?"

Tito answered, "Yeah, my homegirl needs a paramedic a.s.a.p., she's unconscious. She was shot in the shoulder and stomach. She's still breathing though."

Ms. Ramirez asked, "Did you throw out all the guns?"

Tito said, "I threw the gun out already, Yang's gloc. Alex had a 38 Revolver-did you find it yet? He killed Yang with it."

Ms. Ramirez said, "We'll talk about all that later. Right now, we have to get you out of there safely. Are you hurt or shot?"

Tito said, "Yeah I'm shot, but nothing major. Look, we got Angela lying on a blanket and we'll pick it up and carry her out to the grass then lay down, is that cool?"

Ms. Ramirez answered, "Yes that sounds perfect Tito. The officer has already picked up the other gloc. Are you sure you don't have any other weapons in there Tito?"

Tito ignored the question and answered, "Alright, I'm on my way out," and he hung up the phone.

Ms. Ramirez had a worried look on her face. Tito put the 12 Gauge Mossberg by the door frame- easily accessible and within reach and opened the front door. Ester was holding two corners of the blanket, backing up out the door as Tito held the other two corners as they carried Angela out. When that door opened every single cop's gun was cocked back simultaneously. Death echoed in the air. The Grim Reaper's presence was felt no doubt.

They were all out the door when Angela started having a seizure, moving and shaking uncontrollably.

Ester's hands were slipping and she was losing her grip when she cried out, "Stop moving Angela, we're trying to get you help," as she tried to keep ahold of the blanket.

Then all of a sudden, Ester's grip was lost and Angela fell to the ground. Tito swiftly squatted down to catch her and shots rang out! Poof! Rata tat tat tat tat!

Alex Lara hit his target, but not where he had wanted. Tito flew backwards into the house and Ester ran with her hands up back towards the house and made it back in.

Sgt. Garza was yelling, "Cease fire! Cease fire!"

Sgt. Travis was also ordering his men to stop shooting. Every cop there had let off some rounds in the chaotic commotion, even though they weren't sure if Tito had pulled a gun out of the blanket and started shooting or what had happened. They'd heard shots and reacted back with rapid gunfire. When all was quiet, Tito heard Sgt. Garza yelling at his men. Tito grabbed the 12 Gauge Mossberg and crawled with Ester back into the restroom.

She was terrified and was trembling and crying. "What about

Angela babe? Angela's out there, do you think they killed her?"

Tito was bleeding something horrible but was checking Ester's body out, getting his blood all over her. He was confused himself, not knowing if she was shot or if it was his own blood that was on her. He asked her, "Are you shot mija? You okay?"

Ester checked out her body. "Is that my blood? Oh my God Tito your fingers are shot off Tito…"

Lucky Tito was in a world of hurt and pain but he came back at her with a sick humor, "All fingers are gone but my middle finger… so I can tell the D.A. fuck you bitch! Fuck this shit hurts," he complained. "Give me a towel or something! Shit I'm leaking gacho!"

Lucky put his hand under the water in the bathtub. Tito was now scared out of his mind, screaming in pain, sounding like an injured lion in the wild. Ester then wrapped up his hand in the bloody towel and they sat against the tub as Ester cried into his chest.

"Angela, oh my God, did they kill Angela? They tried to kill us Tito. We didn't even do nothing! Why Lucky why?" She cried.

Lucky Tito was sweating bullets. "The pigs are on some hater shit. They want me dead, not you. Look, I bled through the towel, it's soaked. I'm gonna bleed out. Fuck man, think, think, think. Man these motherfuckers got me fucked up and twisted. I haven't killed a cop yet, but I'm going out blasting next time. Fuck the pigs! You gotta stay in the restroom when I go out blasting," he told Ester.

She was crying and she kissed Tito and begged him, "No mijo, no don't do it! Please I don't want you to die. Please!"

Tito said, "If I go out and they kill me, you'll live. All they want is me man! Aye check it out-just go get me my syringe and a fat piece of Negra. It's on the ashtray. I need to kill this pain."

Ester just sat there in shock. She was scared but admired how Lucky Tito Lopez was willing to sacrifice his own life to save hers.

Tito said, "Snap out of it, get the dope and rig. This shit hurts like a mu fucka."

Ester did as she was told while Tito re-wrapped his injured hand and sat on the toilet. She came back with a full syringe of heroin. It was thick black and it looked like a burnt demon. Ester slammed it into Tito's neck and he head rushed.

"Yeah, yup, yup, that's it. Told you this is some bomb black shit! I'm gonna catch this mutha fuckin dragon one day watch Ester." He belched like he was gonna throw up.

Ester moved back away from him saying, "Eww don't barf on me." She knew he was really loaded as he went instantly into a nod. He was out of it. Ester noticed he was bleeding through his boxers, so she pulled the waistband of his pants down and saw that his hip had been hit, and badly. She did what she could to clean away the blood. As Tito came back out of his nod he felt his high was gone and he knew that he was weakening. At the same time, Ester was thinking that she wasn't going to slam anymore shit.

Denise Lopez was yelling and cursing at Sgt. Garza and Sgt. Travis, "You lied; you can't even control your own men! You wanna kill someone, then kill me you bastard!"

She slapped Sgt. Garza, then turned and walked right through the maze of cop cars, into the yard and up to the front door of the house. She opened the front door and walked into the house. Cops yelled at her to come back, but she ignored them and pushed them away from her knowing damn well that her son wouldn't shoot her.

Ms. Ramirez was yelling at Sgt. Garza, giving him orders to cuff Officer Alex Lara and put him in the backseat of his own cop cruiser. Sgt. Garza did just that and confiscated Lara's weapons.

Ms. Ramirez got in her car and parked it on the side of Lara's car where he was cuffed up yelling, "You don't got nothing on me stupid bitch. I was doing my job!"

Ms. Ramirez said, "You're the bitch and I'm fucking you in the ass this time! You can kiss your job goodbye Lara! Trust that you're going to prison just as soon as I figure this all out!"

She walked away and Alex Lara had to admit that her ass looked cute in her black and white pin striped suit. He threw a kiss at her as he yelled, "Fuck you bitch!"

Denise Lopez was in the dark house carefully walking through glass and blood. "Tito where are you," she called out as she turned down the dark hallway. "Tito where are you son?"

Tito jumped up pointing the gun at his mother, half out of his mind. He tried to pull the trigger but the gun slipped out of his bloody hand and the 12 Mossberg fell to the floor, accidentally going off into the dry wall.

Ester yelled, "Tito, don't it's your mom!"

He tried to pick up the 12 gauge then said, "WHAT? Mom, my mom...Naw serio?" He turned on the restroom light so he could see down the hall.

His mom was ducking down on her knees with her hands over her head. "Don't shoot mijo, it's me okay?" she yelled out.

Tito tried to walk to her but fell back down on the toilet. "Moms come here, why you here?" he cried.

Denise Lopez made her way into the bathroom, knelt down next to her son and started examining him. She could see that he was badly hurt. She knew he was discombobulated though mostly from the heroin, when she saw the syringe. She checked out his wounds and hugged him, kissing the top of his head, patting his back and shoulders.

Tito slurred, "How'd I get into this mess moms? I just wanted to score a little dope, then one thing lead to another. Wrong place, wrong time I guess. I never thought nothing like this would happen." He cried in frustration as Denise caressed her son's head, rocking him back and forth, kneeling in front of him.

"It's okay, it's okay. I'm not going to let them kill you. Before they kill you, they have to kill me first. We're going out together, and I'm going to be in front. Hug me from behind and have your friend hug you," she told Tito.

The phone rang and Ester ran into the living room and picked it up and yelled, "What the fuck aye! We trusted you and you tried to kill us!"

Ms. Ramirez was on the line and said, "Those orders were not from me or the bosses. Officer Lara shot at Tito and the rest of the officers followed suit. It won't happen again, I swear. Can I talk to Tito?" Ester walked back towards Tito and handed him the phone.

He talked weakly into the receiver, saying, "What aye?"

Then Ms. Ramirez repeated to him what she'd told Ester but she added, "Tito, Alex Lara is cuffed up in the cop car right now and he'll pay for what he did to you. He WILL be going to jail. Can I come in and talk to you?"

Tito said, "Yeah, I gotta gauge but I aint trippin on you."

Denise picked up the guage, grabbed the phone away from Tito and said, "I've got the gun so you don't have nothing to worry about. Come on in."

Denise handed the phone back to Tito and he told Ms. Ramirez, "Do you hear that? Moms got the gauge," he laughed deliriously into the phone.

Ms. Ramirez said, "Throw the unloaded gun out the door Tito."

Tito shook his head and answered, "Nope that ain't happening. You wanted me to trust you and I did and ended up shot. Now you trust me, take a chance. I'm not talking about it no more. Come on in, come in empty handed, I'm waiting."

Ms. Ramirez wasn't sure how to take that. She scratched her head thinking it over. Was it a threat or should she take a chance. Now she was playing Russian roulette. She knew Tito was pissed off and severely stressed out of his mind. *Is this a trick?* She asked herself. She had a life or death decision to make.

Tito mumbled to Ester, "Get...get the umm... key box, show moms, attic for duffle."

Denise softly patted Tito's cheeks telling him, "Wake up mijo, stay awake." She looked over at Ester and asked her, "How much Black has he used today?"

Ester shrugged her shoulders, feeling uncomfortable talking to Tito's mom about his dope usage. She folded her arms when she noticed Denise checking out her track marks.

Ester broke eye contact and began wetting a towel for Tito and then answered, "I don't know how much shit he's done. Maybe three shots since he got here. He's been chewing nonstop on morphine pills too. I know he's hella messed up."

Denise said, "No shit, he looks half dead."

Ester just walked away and went and got the house key. She called Denise to the room and gave the key to her, showed her where the attic was and told her about the duffle bag. "There's money and heroin in there. You can come back here when we're in jail and get the bag of money, but just leave the heroin alone because it's mine and I owe someone for it," she lied. She knew Tito would need more money and figured she could sell some of it for him once she got out.

Denise just looked at Ester sideways, doubting her lies as she saw right through her. She thought to herself, *This girl is out of her fricken mind if she thinks I'm gonna come up in here and...* There was a knock on the front door that interrupted her thoughts and she walked in that direction saying, "I got it."

Ester went back into the restroom and patted Lucky Tito's forehead with a wet towel. She picked up the 12 gauge and jacked it off, cocking one shell into the chamber of death.

Tito wickedly grinned and opened his eyes reaching for it when he heard the sound. Ester handed the 12 gauge to him and helped him to put his shot, wrapped hand underneath the gun while with his good hand he gripped the pistol grip with his finger on the trigger. "That's my girl. Fuck the police," he said as he ducked his head down and closed one eye, aiming the gauge down the dark hallway. He let out a sick, evil growl "Grrrr, hahaha. It ain't no fun when the rabbit gots the gun mu fuckas."

Ms. Ramirez turned the corner leading into the dark hallway. There at the end of the hall was the restroom and in the dimly lit area she saw a bloody demon pointing her death sentence right at her. She instantly froze, putting her hands up and whining, "No mo…!"

Right at that very moment Ms. Ramirez became a believer in God and started praying as hard as she could to Him. She saw the devil in flesh form and knew that since there really was a devil, there had to be a God.

Ester was standing at Tito's side with her hand on his shoulder, supporting his decision. Why not? They'd tried to kill them both. Shoot, the Bible says, an eye for an eye, tooth for a tooth. Either way, this was God's wrath or the Devil's terror, depending on your views and beliefs; also, what side of the black barrel you're on.

Ms. Ramirez fell down on her knees. "No Tito, no please, I'm here to help you…pleeaasse," she bowed down begging.

Denise's voice snapped Tito out of his trance and he was no longer demon possessed like Damian. Denise moved in front of Ms. Ramirez and told her son, "Don't do it Tito! Put the cuete down mijo, do it for me."

Lucky Tito looked up at Ester, who said, "You can't with your mom there, hear her out, fuck it."

It took all of Tito's energy to hold that gauge up. He finally put it down at his side, but still held on to it.

His mother confidently walked towards him as if she was 187 proof and couldn't be murdered. She knew that her son would not murder her. Now the cops, that was a different story because they were unpredictable. Ms. Ramirez shakily stood up and followed Denise into the restroom. She stood in the doorway and Denise went over and sat on the tub. Ester was still at Tito's side, wiping away the blood and sweat on his forehead.

Lucky Tito ordered, "Strip down Ramirez, what I gotta do, you do too. Fair is fair and you better not have a gun, I ain't asking twice either."

Ms. Ramirez licked her lips as she nervously waited for Denise or Ester to intervene, but they didn't and Tito gripped the gauge and began pulling it upwards again when she didn't move.

Then Ramirez said, "I don't have any weapons Tito, I'm trusting you, so trust me." She unbuttoned her black and white pin striped suit jacket, took it off and gave it to Ester who searched it. Ramirez was wearing a white silky blouse and her tits were voluptuous. Her body was sexy as fuck and she was just gorgeous.

Tito whistled checking her out. "Damn it Ramirez, I don't even remember you being this fine. I'm gonna enjoy this, any chance I could get a lap dance?" he laughed.

Denise giggled nervously, trying to break the tension in the air and thinking, even *through all this hell Tito is going through, and he's still flirting and joking.*

Tito noticed her empty, brown shoulder holster and ordered her to turn around in a full circle. She did as she was told, then began unbuttoning her blouse.

Tito said, "As tempting as it is, I'd love to see the strip show, but your clothes are so tight I can see you have no guns, you're straight. So what's the plan cuz I can't think of nothing to do, my brain hurts as much as the rest of my body. I've been beat all day."

Ms. Ramirez noticed the syringes and dope on the counter and said, "That smack don't help either Tito."

Tito laughed saying, "How do you know, have you tried it? It's helping me right now, taking all my pain away, both physical and mental. Matter of fact, fuck talking about it ima' *be* about it. You're gonna do a shot, then tell me if you think it's bad."

Denise said, "Tito, what's wrong with you, I didn't raise you like this! Ramirez is here to help you and you're trippin on her, just stop that shit. You're not shootin no one and you're not slammin no dope in no one either. That's how you got in this mess in the first place! Now you're acting like your father."

Tito waved his mom off, scratching his head and nose, saying, "Whatever, I'm not like that asshole. I gotta fever but I'm freezing and I feel sick again. I need a fix Ester, get me a shot."

Denise and Ramirez both spoke, "I don't think it's a good idea Tito," Ramirez said.

"No mijo, we're going to go out right now and let the paramedics work on you," Denise told him.

Tito started rotating his neck and shaking his wounded foot and said, "My leg's numb, it feels asleep."

Ms. Ramirez was trying to take control of the situation without offending Tito or coming off too strong by giving him orders. Her training told her that she had to be subtle and not aggressive. She knew that she had to make suggestions and give Tito options, so it would seem like he was the one in control, calling the shots. Ms. Ramirez made a hand sign at Denise, pointing to the gun, while Tito had his eyes closed in a heroin nod. Denise shook her head yes, understanding that she was asking her to help get the weapon from Tito. This would give Ramirez the edge she needed to get them all out safely.

Ester was on point though and had Tito's back. "Wake up Tito, come on babe, stay alert," she told him, pulling his head up to face Ms. Ramirez.

Ramirez shook her head as though saying NO and then threw her hands up in the air disgustedly as if saying, what's up!

Ester just looked at her and said, "Nothing's up. You ain't getting the gun, fuck that, just back the fuck up!"

Hearing that, Lucky Tito squeezed the gun up to his chest and put it on his lap, then said, "Ester, turn the music on babe, I need some music on to help me think."

Ester went to the restroom counter and pressed play on the CD player.

Tito said, "Turn it full blast, Ramirez might be wired or have a bug or somethin," he laughed saying, "matter fact on second thought, a strip tease sounds good right about now, check for wires."

Ester brought Tito a cup of water and he downed it, but felt like he was going to barf again.

Tito shook it off saying, "Oh that's my shit right there, Brotha Lynch^v spits that sick shit."

Tito started throwing up gang signs and stuck his middle finger out, dissecting the lyrics and flowing them like a drunk ass fool. He felt like he could relate to the lyrics, like Lynch was rapping about him. He was hearing subliminal messages in the lyrics as he chewed on a few more pills, chasing them down with some water.

Tito rapped Lynches lyrics,
"I was a dead man walking they say,
So every night I hit the J,
Load the A.K. and post up
In the window till come day
Anyway, hey I feel the payback
Simmerin in my brain
Thoughts of death cloud my mind
As my niggas is gone away
Many clips and 24 riches but who really gots ma back...
Cause its EBK all day, every day
Til the day I die
I'm creepin through yo set with a mini Mack 10,
A-R-ONE-5 Rugga
With a 12 gauge pump in the trunk"...

He stopped rapping Brotha Lynch's lyrics and picked up the 12-gauge pump, waving it up in the air and saying, "That's right, fools spittin at me!" This murder mission music was hyping Tito up to go against the grain and go out shooting. In the lyrics, EBK means Every Body Killa.

That's the last thing Ms. Ramirez wanted. She didn't want his mind frame in kill mode. Denise picked up on the vibes, walked over and turned off the CD player.

Tito complained saying, "Man what the hell, I was slappin that shit, it's a banger."

Denise said, "Man up before I slap you Tito, and give me the gun!"

She reached for it as Ms. Ramirez said, "Empty all the shells first Tito."

Lucky Tito pulled the 12 gauge out of his mother's reach then ordered, "Everyone go to the living room, come on, let's go!" Then he stood up and using the gauge as a cane, he limped down the hallway, following the girls and saying, "Fuck this shit hurts Ester!"

Ms. Ramirez again asked him to empty the gauge but Tito just smiled at her and told her that since she had asked him so nicely, he would meet her halfway. Then he handed the black Mossberg to Ester and told her to, "Empty it all except for one shell."

Ester jacked the pistol grip and red shells fell to the floor one at a time. She checked the chamber, saw, and showed Tito the last one left. He told her that was excellent and then whispered in her ear as she handed the gauge to him. Ester then walked back down the hallway. Ms. Ramirez and Denise were clueless. What part of the game was this?

Ramirez nervously asked, "Who's the last shell for Tito?" She picked up the other shells and put them in her jacket pocket as Tito laughed wickedly. That laugh even gave his mother chills up her spine and arms. Denise rubbed her arms to warm up and shake it off.

Tito just ignored Ramirez's question but said, "The plan is, you'll take Ester and my mom out first, then you'll come back for me."

He smiled and Ms. Ramirez asked again, "So who's the last shell for Tito?"

He looked down the barrel of the gun laughing and replied, "Me." Then he pointed it at Ms. Ramirez, who stepped back, and he said, "Or maybe you, it all depends."

Lucky Tito seemed demon possessed again. His eyes looked black, hollow and soulless. Ms. Ramirez was so terrified she almost pissed in her pants. Her life was flashing by.

Tito was unpredictable and full of extreme aggression.

FOUL BALL
PRESENT DAY, MAY 5TH, 2008-10:29 A.M.

Zoe pulled up to the carnival and arranged with a friend of the family to take care of Frankie-boy. He was having so much fun and did not even know what his father was going through. Zoe kissed him goodbye and then drove to Redlands. When she got there, she found a big scene of cops and news camera crews and she could feel the tension in the air. Although the area was cordoned off with yellow crime scene tape, she was able to get through and find Tina and the pastors. Tina was tripping because she didn't want to see Tito die and she had a bad feeling in her gut. She was also pissed off at Tito because she knew that the house Tito was in was his sancha Ester's pad. One day awhile back, when he had been loaded and feeling bad about cheating on her, he had confessed to Tina that he'd been messing around with Ester. Tito had promised Tina that he'd never see her again and Tina had made Tito take her to Ester's house and forced Tito to tell Ester that it was over between them.

Ester had told Tina, "Go ahead and think that bitch, Tito's just as much mine as he is yours so get over it."

Tina wasn't putting up with Ester's disrespect so she bum rushed Ester and they fought it out in the front yard for a good half hour.

They took rest breaks and everything. They were both hoodrats raised in the barrio, so their skills were up to par and they fought like gangster ass fools. There was some hair pulling but mostly fists and kicking. While they fought, a circle of gangsters stood around them drinking, cheering and enjoying the show. It was about even when all was said and done, and Tito had promised never to see Ester again. Now he was posted up hiding in her house, so Tina had mixed emotions. She was mad at Tito, yet scared for him.

Zoe sat in the backseat with Tina, they hugged each other tightly and Zoe said, "I talked to my boss and he said that he'll represent Tito. He's the best there is. He says he'll plead not guilty by reason of temporary insanity on Tito's behalf. He thinks Tito had a mental breakdown due to Alex pushing him over the edge by setting him up. He'll probably do less than ten years in Patton State Hospital. We've just gotta get him out of there first," Tina said.

Officer Alex Lara was sitting in the back of his cop car with his hands cuffed up in front of him. He was still able to reach in the seat and pull out the throw away 22 Caliber that he had stashed there earlier. He had a couple of 22 bullets in his back pocket, but it was going to be mission impossible to reach them, being that his hands were cuffed up in front. He was racking his brain trying to figure out a way to reach them when he noticed Olga Olspina walking towards him. Alex Lara saw her cameraman following her, bright lights and all, so he hid the 22 pistol between his legs. The window of the cruiser was three quarters of the way up, slightly open for fresh air and Olga approached and stuck her mike through the window and asked Alex, "Do you care to make a comment as to why you're under arrest officer?"

Lara said, "All I gotta say is that Tito Lucky Lopez murdered my partner, Officer Yang, this morning in the city of Colton. He also murdered a Crip named Rasheed Thomas, which we believe was gang related. He also murdered a Mexican Mafia member in San Bernardino and robbed a store and a bank. He also shot me when I tried to arrest him. HE'S the bad guy and I'm the one being targeted by Internal Affairs. This isn't right!"

Officer Lara figured he would start the trial by media process already and smut Tito up so that possible future jurors and viewers would have a negative view of Tito Lopez before the trial even started. This way they would hang Tito and acquit him. Olga Olspina moved the microphone closer as Alex spoke.

After hearing his comment, she felt sorry for Officer Lara and said, "My condolences on the loss of your partner, officer," and she walked away. Lara smiled thinking, 'Gotcha Tito!'

As soon as she walked off, he reached for his back pockets trying to get the bullets. He still was not able to get them out of his pocket so he just put the 22 pistol on the side of his leg so that he would have easy access to it. Lara's mind was racing 100 miles per hour as he talked to himself like a nutcase.

SACRIFICE BUNT
PRESENT DAY, MAY 5TH, 2008-10:45 A.M.

Denise walked up to her son, hugged him and said, "You better not kill yourself or I'll kick your ass Tito. Don't talk like that mijo."

Tito answered, "Okay ma but when them pigs put bullets in my back you're gonna be the one wiping my ass cuz I'm crippled. Are you gonna do that?"

Denise said, "I'll die for you so stop asking dumb questions. You got an officer in here and the cops aren't gonna shoot with her as a shield."

Ester walked back into the living room and winked at Tito saying, "It's done babe, get yours whenevers."

Tito hugged Ester whispering in her ear again, "Remember, bring that sack to court, I'll get it on the bus."

Ester whispered back, "I told your mom not to touch the heroin, that it's mine, but I'll sell it for you so you got money."

They kissed each other and Tito coughed holding his good hand over his bruised ribs to help the pain. When Yang had kicked him he had broken them, and with each cough, Tito felt a stabbing pain shoot through his body.

A little blood leaked out of his mouth and Ester wiped it away saying, "You need a doctor babe."

Tito just pushed her and his mom towards Ramirez ordering, "Put one under each wing Ramirez and roll out. I'll be in the window with the gauge pointing at your back Ramirez and if the pigs shoot I'm taking you out and comin out buckin an empty gun."

Denise said, "You don't got murder suicide in your blood Tito, quit talking like that!" She turned around, kissed her son and said, "God bless you mijo, I love you. I'll see you in a few. It'll be okay, everything is going to be okay Tito."

Then, all three women walked out of the front door. Tito mumbled to himself, *I got suicide, murder and heroin in my blood moms, I'm not your little boy anymore.*

He had the 12 Gauge Mossberg pointed right at Ms. Ramirez's back. Tito was so out of it though that he didn't even realize that if he shot at Ramirez's back, the BB's would expand and also hit Ester and his mother.

As soon as the women walked out three cops ran up on Ester and cuffed her, then escorted her to a cop car. Ms. Ramirez waved the cops away from Denise Lopez when they tried to cuff her, but she ordered her to step back away. Ms. Ramirez's back was facing Tito and Sgt. Garza was standing in front of Ramirez. All Tito could really see was Garza's head.

Ramirez put on a jacket and whispered to the Sargent, "Garza is Tito looking at me?"

Sgt. Garza answered, "Like an eagle."

Ms. Ramirez said, "Casually pull your gun and give me a hug and slide the gun into my shoulder holster. He's on one Garza, he's psychotic and losing his mind. He's hallucinating and unpredictable. He has a gauge with one shell and he wants me to go back in and escort him out."

Sgt. Garza hugged her and slickly slid his gun in her holster and said, "Don't go back in, we'll just raid with bulletproof shields. You said he only has one shell."

Ms. Ramirez turned to face Tito and saw him close the blinds, but didn't know if he had moved away from the window. She said, "He might have more shells in the house and might be loading up as we speak. I'm going back in before he has a chance to reload. He's injured so it'll take him a few minutes."

Ms. Ramirez was trying to be brave, but she really did not want to go back inside because she was full of fear. The definition of bravery to her though was facing her fears and walking through her fears in order to overcome those fears. She reached into her holster, acting as though she had an itch, and took the safety off the 40 gloc so that it would be ready to blast. One thing she wasn't was a coward.

Tito was in the restroom in bad shape, but his mind was still focused on getting high. That's the mentality of a hooked dope fiend. Their life revolves around getting high, even during life and death situations. Lucky Tito Lopez had turned the radio on again and was listening to,

The Art Laboe Oldie but Goodie Show. He heard a slow song playing that reminded him of his father. The songs' title was, *"Somebody Please."* For some reason Lucky Tito climbed into the bathtub and lay down. It was as if Tito was reenacting the scenario that had happened when he was twelve. Like the night that his father beat him and forced his first shot into him. He sure felt beat up just like he had that day 22 years ago. Tito lay in the tub with the 12 gauge on his lap and slammed a thick full syringe shot into his neck veins. There was a little hand mirror close by and he picked it up and stared at himself.

He was startled as he realized that he now looked exactly like his father. Tito was 34 years old and still had his golden heart full of love for others. His drug addiction is what had him twisted. He had tried kicking the dope but it was too strong and it had a hold of him. He was obsessed with catching that black dragon because he figured that once he caught the dragon he'd have the ultimate high and no more pain. Then he'd be set free of his addiction. An older dope fiend had told him that story when he was 13 years old and he'd been chasing that dragon ever since. He'd get higher and higher trying to catch him, but the dragon always managed to fly even higher and he could never catch up. It had cost Tito a lot of time and heartache.

Tito was lost in the lyrics of the oldie song, *"Somebody Please."* He actually understood each word and as he listened to the lyrics this time, he pictured his father on his knees, crying and burning in the pits of hell. He tried to sing along as the song played,

"Somebody please... give me just a minute,
To explain... my misery...oh somebody please,
Won't you help me...can't you see the fire
burning, can't you see the wheels are turning... "[vi]

Tito thought, *Yeah pops, I can see the fire burning. I wish somebody would please help me too pops.*

Ms. Ramirez crept into the restroom and saw Tito pulling the syringe out of his neck and wiping the blood away. He had closed his eyes when he felt the rush and dizziness overtake him as his heartbeat had slowed down and he didn't even notice her there.

Ms. Ramirez reached down and grabbed the nine gauge, cocked it back and the shell fell out. She threw the empty gun out into the hallway then she grabbed the syringe and threw it into then the toilet. She leaned over and helped Tito, throwing his arm over her shoulder and telling him, "Come on Tito it's over, let's go. Everything is going to be okay now, I've got your back and no one's going to shoot you."

Tito was groggy and half out of it muttering, "Aye Ramirez, you know my dream was to be a Colton cop? I liked their bulletproof vests and helmets. I wanted to earn it. I had dreams Ramirez. This heroin fucked me all up. My dad did this to me. He was supposed to love me and take care of me."

He hopped along with tears falling leaking down his face and mumbling, "What's up with that? That aint right huh? Que gacho, que no? Aye guess what... can you believe Alex... Alex Lara... used to be my best friend; we were going to join the academy together. But I went to youth authority instead. I couldn't let them homos hurt my sister."

Ms. Ramirez led Tito out the door and towards a waiting cruiser. He was blind to the crowd of cops and cameras around him and was talking to Ramirez as if it was just the two of them strolling through the park.

Ramirez asked him, "So you and Alex used to be best friends?"

"Yup, yup, he was my dog," he answered.

Ms. Ramirez said, "Wow, with friends like that, who needs enemies. Okay Tito I'm going to put you in the car now and drive you to the hospital."

Tito opened up his swollen eyes, looked up and saw that he was surrounded by cops who were mean mugging him as if they wanted to kill him. He shouted out, "What you putos looking at, you had your chance!"

Ms. Ramirez decided to cuff Tito's hands up in front of him because of his hand wound. She felt sorry for him, which was unusual for her and not at all professional. There was something about the whole experience that had rattled her. She was feeling dangerously close to Tito. There was a thin line between them and honestly, at that point she totally related to Tito and just wanted to get him to the hospital and get him all the help she could. She tried to shrug off the sadness she was feeling and walked away, taking a deep breath as she made her way back over to the other side.

Tito was laid out in the back seat of the cruiser, drifting in and out of consciousness as the drugs flowed through his veins. Then he heard Tina's voice and he managed to pull himself up. He saw her standing there looking in at him through the partially opened window.

She was crying and she asked him, "Tito are you okay babe? What did they do to you?"

Tito laughed half-heartedly so that Tina wouldn't be worried, then said, "I'm alright babe. These pigs can't fade me. It's nothing, Ima' shake it off like nada. Go to the hospital babe."

Tina tried to reach in to give him a kiss but a cop saw her, grabbed her by the arm and told her that she wasn't supposed to be there and moved Tina away from the cruiser. She was heartbroken but she decided to get back to the car so she could go to the hospital as Tito had asked her to do.

As Tito watched her walk away, he saw something from the corner of his swollen eyes. Tito saw Alex cuffed up in a cop car five feet away from where he was. Then Tito really started laughing.

He yelled, "Oh hell Yeah it's on now Alex! You're gonna be in my cell and bitch punk I'll see you in the county for sure that. Yup, yup, it's goin down! There's nowhere to run now puto!"

Alex Lara spit out the window towards Tito and yelled, "Fuck you Tito!"

Tito ducked back and laughed in a frenzy, but he started coughing up blood so he just lay back down. He was exhausted but he felt somewhat relieved. "I'll N-S-C- your bitch ass at West Valley punk, CHOWWWWW, CHOWWWW!" Tito howled.

Hearing all the commotion, everyone turned to see what was going on and they heard Tito yelling, "Ramirez I caught the dragon by his damn tail, it's over, it's really over! No more pain."

He took a deep breath and slumped over sideways, leaning against the door as he mumbled to himself, *it's okay now, everything's okay.*

Ms. Ramirez had walked back over to the cruiser when she heard Tito yelling her name. She figured Tito was hallucinating and spoke to him through the window saying, "Okay Tito that's good, take a nap and relax. You're going to be okay Tito; everything is going to be all right."

Tito smiled at her and then rolled over sideways, closed his eyes and lay down.

A few minutes later, Tina felt as though something in her soul wasn't right. She made her way back over to the cop car Tito was in, pushing through cops and cameramen.

"Tito!" she yelled loudly, "Tito, are you okay?" Tina tapped on the window trying to get Tito to respond and kept yelling his name but he never responded. Then she started to scream, "Tito wake up babe, wake up!"

Hearing this, Ms. Ramirez quickly walked over, opened the back door of the cruiser and looked in at Tito. She saw that his skin was a purplish color. He was slumped over sideways and his lips were curled upward in a peaceful looking grin. She quickly pulled his shackled wrists towards her and checked for a pulse. But there was none. Then she put her ear to his bloody chest, listening for his heartbeat. When she didn't hear one, Ms. Ramirez dragged Tito out of the car, laid him on the ground and desperately began giving him CPR. Tina screamed as Ms. Ramirez sat on Tito and started pounding on his chest with her clenched fists, then began pummeling him like a punching bag and slapping him across his cheeks. She grabbed him by the shoulders and wildly started shaking his limp body, trying to wake him.

By then the paramedics had rolled over to area with lights flashing. They tried to place Tito onto the stretcher, but Ms. Ramirez, who was in a frenzy, hindered their efforts. She was still sitting on him, straddling him like a horse and was vainly trying to blow some life back into his battered body. They could not pry her loose, so they placed Tito with Ms. Ramirez still sitting on top of him, onto the stretcher and rolled them both into the waiting vehicle.

Denise was in a daze. She was crying and trembling as she leapt up into the ambulance with Tito and Ms. Ramirez. Tina was just barely able to lean into the ambulance and grab Tito's limp, manacled hands, kiss them and say," I love you babe, God bless you."

Then the ambulance sped off with sirens screaming, wailing off into the night, but Tina knew it was too late. She had already felt her soul mate's soul leave her heart. She was calm but stunned, almost tranquilized.

Lucky Tito Lopez had overdosed. Tito's luck had finally worn off and he was already dead in the street.

Officer Alex Lara was in the back seat of the cruiser, laughing his ass off. "Ha-ha! Die motherfucker die! You son of a bitch! That's what you get, you dope fiend. You're so stupid you killed yourself you idiot. Go to hell you piece of shit. Looks like you finally ran out of luck huh Lucky? Hahaha," He laughed maniacally.

Tina casually strolled over to the cop car Alex Lara was in and looked around at the crowd of people and law enforcement.

Olga Olspina's cameraman aimed his camera on Officer Alex Lara, who was clearly making an ass of himself. He was acting unprofessionally, almost like the criminals he had set up over the years.

There was a cop guarding Alex Lara, but he was just sitting on the trunk smoking a cigarette, paying attention to the crowd. He hadn't even noticed when Tina walked up to the car. Tina's eyes were saddened. Tears were pouring down her cheeks as she walked up to the window where Alex sat. When he did notice her he told her to back up and walked over to push her away. Lara knew the cop and said, "Buddy, lemme have a moment partner." He winked at the guard who sat back down on the trunk of the police cruiser.

Tina stared at Lara and said, "You think Tito's dying is funny huh?" She glared at Alex Lara with a heart full of rage and hate.

Alex Lara laughed and said, "Yeah that shit's funny you dumb bitch. You like playing with hearts, well live with that shit. I know it broke your heart. The funny part is that I drove Tito to kill himself. Hahaha!"

Tina replied, "Keep laughing asshole. You'll die on death row Alex, and I'll be watching with a smile on my face!"

Corrupt Officer Alex Lara spit at Tina, "Is that right?" he said as he reached for the 22 pistol that he'd stashed. He pointed it at Tina saying, "How about I kill you right now so you can go to Hell with fuckin Tito?"

Tina was stone-faced and didn't even flinch at his hateful words. She wasn't afraid of dying. Tina knew that she had Alex Lara's heart and love, so if he shot her, it would be as if he was shooting himself in the heart. She glared at him and said, "You're a pussy Alex!"

She turned her back on him and had only taken five steps when Alex began laughing again, "Hahaha, fuck Tito bitch!"

Tina, in one swift motion, quickly reached in her bra and pulled out a miniature Chrome North American Dillinger 22 pistol. She ran up to the window and yelled, "Laugh at this motherfucker! Fuck Tito? Naw, fuck you!"

And with that, she unloaded the six 22 Longs, hot bullets into Alex Lara's cold heart and astonished face.

Tina cried out, "That's for Tito. If love don't get ya, hate will kill you-believe that! Go to Hell Alex! Looks like *you* ran out of luck! Three strikes, *you're* out!"

Tina dropped the gun and lifted her hands up in the air. She was quickly taken into custody.

As she was driven to the police station, Tina gazed through the window at the dark angry clouds swirling around the full moon. She imagined Tito and Alex fighting in the sky, their ghosts still battling for her love.

The moon was Tito Lucky Lopez, looking down at her smiling happily. She heard his laugh in her head and his voice saying, *I'm okay now. I'm okay babe.*

She smiled back whispering, "I love you babe. God bless your soul! Walk with the angels my love."

Tears of joy leaked down her face as she realized that her true love, Tito, was no longer addicted and finally was no longer feeling any pain.

EPILOGUE:

Since Zoe's boss had a cash retainer to represent Tito he ended up representing Tina and did an excellent job at it. Tina got a deal for twelve years. Any other criminal would have ended up on death row for killing a cop, but Olga Olspina's cameraman had captured a cuffed Officer Alex Lara pointing a pistol at Tina, that was not an approved police issued one. The tape showed him threatening Tina Lopez's life. The gun Tina had pulled out was registered in her own name. Because of the incident, many questions arose about police corruption within the Colton Police Department. Because of all this, the issue was swept under the rug and Tina took a twelve-year deal that the DA offered her. The investigation found that although Alex Lara's 22 pistol wasn't loaded, he had a back pocket full of bullets. Oh, and a face and heart full of bullets too! Karma's a bitch!

Lucky Tito Lopez passed away tragically, but his trials and tribulations were logged in his journal. Ms. Martinez, his Youth Authority counselor, had shown him how to vent and grieve by keeping a journal. Tito had written his deepest, darkest secrets and thoughts in that journal. He'd written about both good and bad times, lessons learned the hard way, his dreams and desires for himself and his family, and about all of his failures, struggles and obstacles on his path to self-destruction. He wrote all about being a gangster and a drug addict.

The day his son Frankie-Boy was born (Dec. 1st), Tito started addressing his journal logins to Frankie-Boy so that one day when he was old enough, he could read and learn from Tito's words. Tito had planned to give his son the journal when he was around twelve or thirteen years old, depending on how mature he was. Tito had been twelve years old when he got hooked on heroin at his father's hands.

That's around the age when kids begin to pick their own paths and friends. Those choices usually determine where they will end up at during their teenage years; In Juvenile Hall camps or sports camps, attending a friend's funeral or having friends attend their own funeral.

Tito's last login had been on Sunday, May 4th, 2008, the day before he died. It read:

"Frankie-Boy, always remember I love you son. I've been going through hell son since I was a kid and I've been trying to change ever since. It's easier said than done. Everyone seems to have a chance, but few seem to have the opportunity. I feel cursed yet blessed cuz Jesus blessed me with you son. Remember Jesus died so we can live. So live for Him! Walk with your angels. Don't ever be like me. I hate who I am. My heart's in the right place, but my mind is controlled by drugs. Drugs are the devil's tools and toys. They feel good at first, but it's a trick cuz they feel bad later. I can't explain it. Just trust me. Never do drugs. It starts out as fun and games, but slowly turns your life into a living hell. Literally, you start hearing voices, seeing things. Crazy shit. I'm high right now, explaining my hellish world from the inside looking out. Son life is not a game. It's only referred to as a game. It's life or death. Once you lose your life, the game is over. There's no start-over button. There are no referees, just crooked cops. There are no halftimes or time-outs, just doing hard time in prison. My hopes are that by me sharing where I went wrong you learn how to do right. The choices I made, you make the opposite. I've tested the waters with gangs and drugs. All dead ends. No future in it. Keep in mind I was high most of my life and I did wrong for what I believed were the right reasons. I had shit twisted, everything I did was out of love so I thought it was the right thing. From banging to jacking, to provide food or protection for the family. It's crazy son. I'm nodding right now, but know everything I'm saying comes from my heart and that's the only good thing in me. I love you son. God bless you mijo."

Frankie-Boy read this journal message on his thirteenth birthday. After his party, his Grandma Denise and Aunt Zoe gave him his last present in private. It was wrapped up in a box. The journal was dirty and had blood and water spots on it, possibly tears. There was also a photo album that contained pictures of his parents' as they had grown from kids to adults. In the back of the album were newspaper articles of Lucky's licks and arrests and a list of all his crimes. Finally, there was a DVD of the day his father had died. It also contained all of the news footage Fox 11 had captured of the standoff his father had been involved in as well as of his mother killing ex-Officer Alex Lara. It showed Ms. Ramirez trying to save his father's life. It was all there. Frankie-Boy dissected every word in his pop's journal and envisioned everything to the point where he foresaw those same choices and decisions, heading down his path. But he was smart.

Frankie-Boy was now sixteen years old and living with his Aunt Zoe Lopez in a better area of Colton. She was strict with Frankie-Boy, but for the most part, he was a good kid and not a hassle. In fact, Frankie-Boy was a star football player on the Colton High School Varsity team. He was the star quarterback that led his team to win the championship. He still hung out with childhood friends on the north side, but usually with jocks. His best friend Joseph was a running back on the CHS football team. Joseph lived in the Rose Garden Apartments, surrounded by temptation. Joseph and Frankie were on the same level and page as far as drugs went. They were a no-no.

Frankie was sitting outside of the apartments on a crate. He was drinking an Orange Crush soda, watching the kids play kick ball. He remembered the stories in his father's journal that talked about the old days, growing up in those very same apartments. Frankie-Boy daydreamed, imagining he could see his mom and dad's ghosts running around the apartment complex before he was born. He kissed the crucifix that he wore. It had belonged to his father. His father had been given the crucifix and chain when he had been twelve years old. Ironically, his father Tito had been shot the same day. He felt blessed. Wearing it made him feel closer to God and to his father somehow.

Just then, Joseph called out, "Frankie, do you wanna grub a burger?"

Frankie stood up, wiping and dusting off his white Levis and straightening out his crimson and gold football jersey. The kid was built for his age. He walked into the apartment saying, "Naw I'm alright."

Joseph lived with his nineteen-year-old cousin, Travieso. His cousin was a gangster and heroin addict and was very aggressive. He had a rep as a rider. Frankie sat on the couch opposite of 'Travieso' who was slamming heroin. Frankie was shaking his head from left to right with a disgusted look on his face. He made a sound with his lips, "Pshh."

Travieso looked up at Frankie and said, "What puto?" then emptied half the syringe in his arm, wiped the blood away saying, "What's crackin Frankie, do you want half? This shit's bomb ese."

Frankie waved him away saying, "Naw I'm straight. I don't fuck around foo."

Travieso stomped over to him and pushed the syringe up to his face saying, "Stop acting like a pussy. You're gonna do this shot! What,

161

you think you're better than me?"

Frankie remembered what his father had written about his grandfather forcing a shot into Tito. Frankie kicked Travieso in the nuts, buckling him in half on the floor.

Travieso groaned, "What the fuck ese!"

Frankie stood over Travieso fists clenched yelling, "*You're* the pussy letting that dope control you! I aint the one homie. You got me twisted. I don't think I'm better than you but I'm better than that!"

Frankie grabbed the half-full syringe, then emptied and broke it and said, "I'm doing you a favor bro! Don't ever disrespect me, offering me this bullshit heroin again!"

Tension was thick as the two stared at each other.

A car honking outside broke up the moment as Frankie looked outside and saw his Grandma Denise waving at him. He walked up to Joseph, shaking his hand and giving him a *homie-love-hug*. "I'm gone my boy. I gotta go see moms in the joint. She'll be home in two years. Stay strong and sucka free bro!" he said looking disgustedly at Travieso.

He walked out the door and got into the white Cadillac and hugged his grandmother.

Some people may think that exposing his father's faults and life style, not holding back any punches and not sugar coating the story may have been too explicit for a young teen. Some may think the stories were glorifying the gangs and drugs. It all depends on your point of view and on how one relates. Some may even say that knowing all this info would give Frankie an excuse to act out and follow his father's tracks. He lost his father to the Grim Reaper and lost his mother to the prison system. But Frankie-Boy grasped everything correctly. When all was said and done, knowing about Tito Lopez's' fucked up life and death experiences actually helped his son.

Frankie-Boy seemed to break the cycle. To break the drug addiction family curse and that is all that Tito had ever really wanted for his son. Frankie-Boy chose to live a straight life by turning a negative into a positive. Frankie-Boy lived drug free because he chose to. He didn't believe in peer pressure. Most importantly, he stayed sober as a sign of respect for his father's memory. This was also his way of paying tribute to his father and mother. You see, in real life in the hood, in the barrios and the ghettos, there are very few happy endings. The real life characters usually end up in prison or in a grave. But there are a few happy times and precious moments. So when those happy times occurred, he learned to enjoy them. Frankie-Boy refused to play the game, because he had everything to lose. Because of this, you can believe that Lucky Tito's son Frankie-Boy would never hear the judge say to him:

THREE STRIKES, YOU'RE OUT!

THE END

HALFWAY 2 HELL

INTRODUCTION

"Death and life are in the power of the tongue and those who love
it will eat its fruit"
-Holy Bible

"When you feel God's wrath, you feel the devil's fear."
-RedRum the Reaper

My name is irrelevant. *What is* relevant is my message to you. I
could be killed for speaking of the dark ways I am bringing to light. I
am a warrior though, who has never hesitated to fight for my life, and I
will fight the Angel of Death as a warrior does. I have experienced
enough death to appreciate life!

There are millions of serial killers in this world. They all fall into
different classes and calibers, just as there are different levels of
homicide. The serial killers that are usually acknowledged and thrown
on the front page of the newspaper or on TV are the sick perverted
weirdoes. Those killers look and act normal, but in the dark, they rape,
molest and chop up bodies and snack on them on some weirdo cannibal
trip. That's the first type of serial killer. But I'm not talking about
them pieces of shit!

Then there's the citizens trained by the U.S. military-Army, Navy,
Air force, Marines. Those who became soldiers in Vietnam and the
Middle East, killing enemies of the U.S. of A. These soldiers became
serial killers lusting for blood, during war. Yet these serial killers are
looked at as heroes. Why? Because they are killing for our country.
But in reality, they are no different from the actual serial killers I am
going to be talking about.

I've had homeboys join the military and kill for the U.S.A. who had
already killed for my neighborhood before they even went to war. The

U.S.A. war was a breeze for them because as kids they grew up in a barrio warzone, a place where killing was the norm.

On the other side of the coin were the soldiers who were considered normal, having grown up in the suburbs and rich areas of the city. They seemed to come back suffering from post-traumatic stress disorder, being haunted by lost souls or ghosts of the victims they were ordered to kill. Their conscience eats them up. Some commit suicide because they know they killed innocent people at times.

There's very little difference-only a thin line, between those serial killers, and the warrior- serial killers I'm speaking of. The only major difference is that the government's serial killers are a bigger group. They are allowed, even ordered, to kill. They are praised for killing and are not locked up for it, like the actual serial killer I'm talking about.

The law considered a person a serial killer after their third kill. I reached that third kill number before I was even seventeen years old.

I'm now talking about the most dangerous, notorious type of serial killer. The one who is not publically acknowledged as one by the authorities. Why not? So the community doesn't break out into a chaotic panic when they realize that they are surrounded by hundreds and thousands of serial killers, stalking their neighborhoods.

The serial killers are top dog, front of the line. Top of the ladder, king of the hill (of dead bodies stacked up). These killers are molded and shaped into killers by uncles, fathers, cousins, homies, and OG's, who've tasted blood and have killed. Their youngsters watch, learn, and then follow suit at the right time. Violence is fed and instilled into them, along with the hood's ways and traditions of doing thangs, handling *biz-nass*. As they grow up it becomes a normal activity. Killing becomes almost like a sport, you can even say, '*evilly trendy.*'

These young street soldiers kill in packs. As all do, they learn how to master their craft by trial and error. Those who don't learn quickly enough from their mistakes eventually become prison soldiers, and keep killing while locked up.

The ones who master the craft early rise from soldier to warrior status. A warrior automatically knows what to do on murder missions and no longer takes orders. A warrior is wise and bold enough to stalk, hunt, and kill on solo missions. Killers raise these ones. They are raised to kill enemies, even when alone, when his elders or fellow OG's aren't around. He will still strike like a deadly viper. If the enemy slips, he sleeps in eternal darkness point blank, in broad daylight or the darkest of midnights. The job gets done.

This type of serial killer kills for thrills and sometimes is addicted to the lifestyle, getting chills when he kills, head rushing and gaining pleasure from his dirty work. These serial killers live and kill by the G-code they swore by. He's looked up to, respected and feared. This type of serial killer is a neighborhood hero warring on the hood's front lines. Battling in barrio warfare, ghetto warfare. He holds close to heart strict standards and morals, living a disciplined life so as not to make mistakes. One mistake can cost him his freedom, or even his very life. He flirts with death, playing a deadly game of Mexican roulette. Not Russian roulette. The warrior has zero tolerance for disrespect of whom and what he loves and represents. He's a warrior who practices patience. Patience he most likely learned sitting in a cell 24/7, waiting to be released.

This warrior controls and exorcises his demons, and kills in the name of love, loyalty, family, gang, hood, and personal beliefs. Just as the military code is God, Honor, Freedom and Country. This warrior's word is impeccable, and his character can never be assassinated, but only praised as a hood legend, even after he's gone away.

Some of these warriors' hearts wickedly belong to the devil. Those serial killers can't control their demons.

Then there's the warrior whose heart belongs to God, so he follows his heart and believes strongly he can't be wrong for doing so. He believes when you feel God's wrath, you also feel the devil's fear. Therefore, this warrior never hesitates to bring God's wrath down upon the sickos, devils and demons possessed individuals in this wicked world. This warrior serial killer murders those rapists, child molesters and criminals who terrorized their neighborhood's citizens. You could even say this warrior is somewhat of a vigilante.

How could that be wrong? Because the law says so? The Holy Bible, God's word, says THE LAW IS A CURSE (Galatians 3:10-14). Therefore, this warrior's work can't be wrong; someone has to slay these demons, point blank. This warrior serial killer is overlooked at times and he is not acknowledged for what he truly is.

Police sometimes turn a blind eye and show up an hour late to a gang-related murder call, giving this warrior a head start. Police can't stop them all so they just draw drag and show up after the fact to do a half-assed investigation and clean up the mess.

Why, you ask? Because the police can't catch outside serial killers and most of the time they aint willing to try holding a sixteen round 9mm (legally issued weapon), against a warrior serial killer's handful of fifty round clips popping into Uzis, AK-47's, mini-14's, AR-15's,

167

and the rest of the illegally issued weapons that they carry. Therefore, the cops slow drag and side step as these warrior serial killers kill each other.

These warriors do what everyone else wants to do, but are afraid to do. This is not unheard of, but it is unspoken of. That is, until now. It does exist, quiet as kept. The ghettos and barrios are gang infested with these warrior serial killers.

Some of the community knows this because these warriors are people in their families, but they are left out of the loop. Yet some elders are aware of which warriors are the most respected, and they are shown a humble reverence in their presence.

There's no sure way to really know who's who, because there are decoys and then there are the true warriors, the warrior serial killers. There's one thing for sure though, these warriors are looked at by their family members as protectors of the neighborhood. That's why nine out of ten times when the cops come around asking questions and investigating, no one has seen or heard anything. All of a sudden, everyone's blind and deaf. Naw, it's not that. What it is, is that they know if the code of silence is broken, the Grim Reaper warrior will come knocking and kicking in their doors next and hand out a death sentence to the violator.

As these young warriors complete murder missions, they are given praise, respect, and love. OG veteran killers adore them. These warriors are rewarded with money, guns, drugs and anything that individual desires. This warrior is then looked at as an equal in a murder squad, and then they are allowed into a deeper inner circle of killers. He becomes one of the chosen few. He's given honor tattoos and he represents the hood's finest and deadliest, elite caliber of men. He's given the honor and power to play God and decide who lives and who dies.

On the other hand, he can play the Devil role and steal as many souls as possible, until he ultimately meets his own doom. This warrior is given the honor and power to represent his family and his generation as the next battle warrior. It runs deep in the blood of a Mexican warrior. This goes all the way back to the Aztecs.

The Aztec-Mexica warrior's main job was to hunt and protect their land and tribe. Nowadays, the land is called a barrio (neighborhood). Nowadays, a tribe is called a gang or set, klicka, crew, Mafia! Back then, Aztecs battled against other tribes. That's tribe tripping-same as today's set tripping, aka gang battling, or gang banging.

It's in our blood, in our roots to evolve in the same way. This battle within us goes back to when our blood began to mix. I'm talking about when the Europeans invaded our land and the Conquistadors raped, molested, and murdered our women and people. Today's warriors are mixed-bloods (mestizo), half Indian-Mexica blood and half-European blood, natural born enemies.

Within each warrior we have an internal battle constantly going on. It was a bad mixture of blood. It's as if the war between my Aztec-Mexicas and the Conquistadors is still going on inside each modern day warrior. Maybe that's why we're born fighters and protectors. This is the way life is, and even though it is not seen on the surface, it could be considered an underground secret society. It also could be a subconscious instinct that's only discovered and awakened as the warrior is groomed to become that destined serial killer he was meant to be.

After his first intimate kill, he begins to crave and lust for blood, like a vampire. Pulling the trigger over and over again becomes easy and is no longer a challenge; no problem. Then he starts experimenting -- killing by knife, hand-to-hand combat in jail or prison, or on the streets. He begins befriending suicidal individuals and talks them into killing themselves. Pushing them over the edge in psychological warfare, killing with his words, exploring the power the tongue alone holds.

There's 187 ways to murder, choose one.

Then there's the gang hood's dress code, which is mandatory and implemented for this specific reason: to confuse and shake the cops giving chase or doing gang sweeps. The piggies are pressured to gang sweep after so many murders occur in their city. The dress code changes by generation and each hood varies. In my city, our dress codes were mandatory baldheads, baggy khakis, or Ben Davis suits, and dark colors (blue, black, grey, baby blue, crimson and gold). It's considered our uniform.

Say there's approximately eighty street soldiers from my hood. There's..., let me count them real quick-1...2...3...? There's a good fifteen of them that are the actual warrior serial killers, doing 90 percent of the dirty work in the area that's scarin ya.

The other sixty-five soldiers are just decoys-fools who just hang out and party, spray paint on walls, fight with other fools, just doing petty shit. They are decoys to throw the cops off track so when an actual warrior killer works and then runs into a house party or crowd of twenty fools dressed the same way as him, the cops lose sight of the actual suspect. This causes a smoke screen of chaos. Sometimes the real killer is caught-sometimes he's not. It's the luck of the draw and no one really knows because the killings continue. These warriors run in packs, crews, clicks, and tribes, my brother.

If you don't understand by now, I'll be blunt! I'm talking about a secret society member, gang-related, dedicated rider, down for "The Cause" homeboy. I'm talking about a gangsta warrior serial killa!

-Signed by an anonymous 187 G.W.S.K

Holy Bible Psalms- 27:3
"Though an army may encamp against me, my heart shall not fear. However, war may rise against me. In this I will be confident."

RedRum Da Reaper-
"Run from death, never toward it.

1-Hooz possessed-
"Meth awakens the demons in humans."

RED BEANS and DIRTY RICE FOR THE SOUL

COREY 'C-MURDER' MILLER
EUGENE L. WEEMS
CLARKE LOWE

Tread the gutta' life with **C-MURDER** in this gripping compilation of poetry that is deeply rooted in the streets and behind prison walls.

WARNING! May cause a severe reaction or death in people who are square to the game. If an allergic reaction occurs, stop reading and seek emergency counseling from your local priest.

$14.95   98pgs   6x9 Paperback   ISBN: 978-0991238019
Celebrity Spotlight Entertainment, LLC

BOUND BY LOYALTY

COREY 'C-MURDER' MILLER
EUGENE L. WEEMS

The novel that critics across the nation are raving about and people are eager to read.

C-Murder and Weems constructed an elaborate contemporary urban thriller full of twists and false starts. Bound by Loyalty is absolutely chilling and bursting with surprises.

$14.95   280pgs   6x9 Paperback   ISBN: 978-0991238002
Celebrity Spotlight Entertainment, LLC

UNITED WE STAND

A TRIBUTE TO THE AMERICAN FALLEN HEROES
OF THE WAR ON TERRORISM

Eugene L. Weems

United We Stand is a beautiful collection of inspirational artwork and passion-filled poetry created as a living tribute to the American troops who have made the ultimate sacrifice for our country in the war against terrorism.

100% of the proceeds from this book will be contributed to provide care packages for the active duty troops who remain engaged in the war overseas and provide college scholarship trust funds for the children of our American fallen heroes.

$14.95   95 pgs   6x9 Paperback   ISBN: 978-1-4251-9130-6
Available on Amazon.com

PRISON SECRETS

Eugene L. Weems

Once recognized as a ruthless killer and remorseless criminal, Lyle Menendez remains housed in a maximum security correctional facility with other notorious murderers and gang members. In this level 4 maximum security prison, even one of America's most notorious murderers could be victimized. This novel will unlock the doors to all the prison secrets; weapons manufacturing, drug smuggling, prison rapes, gang politics, officer corruption and much, much more.

$14.95   188 pgs   6x9 Paperback   ISBN: 978-0984045662
Available on Amazon.com

AMERICA'S MOST NOTORIOUS GANGS

Eugene L. Weems
Clarke Lowe

For the first time in history America's most notorious gangs: Bloods, Crips, Northerners, Southerners, and Nazis have united for one common purpose. Former members of these violent gangs are making a call for peace, in an attempt to deter At-Risk youth and troubled adults from gangs, violence, drugs, and criminal activities. Their warnings offer a glimpse into the harsh reality of gang life, from the streets to a prison cell. The truth is exposed and the myths are dispelled. In this unique book the authors include motivational commentary, social skill lessons, self assessments and a journal section. These are provided for promoting personal growth, self-worth, accountability and reducing gang participation. The gang prevention and awareness (GPA) lesson plan is presented with the hope of decreasing crime and fostering more positive, productive members of society.

$14.95   167 pgs   6x9 Paperback   ISBN: 978-0984045686
Available on Amazon.com

Celebrity Spotlight Entertainment, LLC
P.O. Box 80724
Bakersfield, California 93380
www.celebrityspotlightentertainmentllc.com

Name:	
Address:	
City:	
State:	Zip Code:
Email:	

QTY	TITLES	PRICE	TOTAL
	Red Beans and Dirty Rice	$14.95	
	Bound by Loyalty	$14.95	
	Innocent by Circumstance	$14.95	
	3 Strikes	$14.95	
	Cold as Ice	$14.95	
	The Green Rose	$14.95	
		Subtotal	
		Shipping	
		TOTAL	

Priority Shipping & Handling: $5.99 for first book, $1.99 each additional book.

The Delfonics, 'La La Means I Love You', copyright 1968,Label: Philly Groove Records pg1150

Al Green, 'How Can You Mend a Broken Heart' lyrics, copyright 1972, Label: Hi Records, written by Barry & Robin Gibb

Etta James, 'I'd Rather go Blind' lyrics, copyright 1968, Label: Cadet Records 5578, writer(s) Ellington Jordan & Billy Foster

Ghetto Heisman,WC, 'Da Get Together',Label: Dub C Online, CAT UMA 1277242243,Release date 2002-11-12

Brotha Lynch, TheRealBrothaLynchHung.com

The Vanguards, 'Somebody Please' lyrics, copyright 1969, Label: Whiz Records Cat # 612